"You've never been upstairs, have you?"

"I've never been invited."

"I'm inviting you now. I even have toothbrushes up there."

"Then it's a done deal."

Still holding Joe's hand, she walked upstairs with him trailing behind her. She didn't say another word, afraid of breaking this spell between them.

Her bedroom door stood open. "You have to see the view."

He stood still at the entrance to the room as she let go and made her way to the windows. Then she heard him whisper across the darkness. "I'm looking at the only view I wanna see right now."

His words sent a thrill through her body.

She stretched out her hands. "Come to me, Red."

She made room for him at the window, and their shoulders nestled together. "Isn't it beautiful?"

He draped his arm over her shoulder and twisted his head to look at her. "The most beautiful view I've ever... Oh, my God, get down!"

And the tender moment ended as glass shattered around them.

DELTA FORCE DIE HARD

CAROL ERICSON

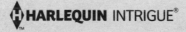

Recycling programs
for this product may
not exist in your area.

ISBN-13: 978-1-335-60412-5

Delta Force Die Hard

Copyright © 2018 by Carol Ericson

All rights reserved. Except for use in any review, the reproduction or utilization of this work in whole or in part in any form by any electronic, mechanical or other means, now known or hereafter invented, including xerography, photocopying and recording, or in any information storage or retrieval system, is forbidden without the written permission of the publisher, Harlequin Enterprises Limited, 22 Adelaide St. West, 40th Floor, Toronto, Ontario M5H 4E3, Canada.

This is a work of fiction. Names, characters, places and incidents are either the product of the author's imagination or are used fictitiously, and any resemblance to actual persons, living or dead, business establishments, events or locales is entirely coincidental.

This edition published by arrangement with Harlequin Books S.A.

For questions and comments about the quality of this book, please contact us at CustomerService@Harlequin.com.

® and TM are trademarks of Harlequin Enterprises Limited or its corporate affiliates. Trademarks indicated with ® are registered in the United States Patent and Trademark Office, the Canadian Intellectual Property Office and in other countries.

Printed in U.S.A.

Carol Ericson is a bestselling, award-winning author of more than forty books. She has an eerie fascination for true-crime stories, a love of film noir and a weakness for reality TV, all of which fuel her imagination to create her own tales of murder, mayhem and mystery. To find out more about Carol and her current projects, please visit her website at www.carolericson.com, "where romance flirts with danger."

Books by Carol Ericson

Harlequin Intrigue

Red, White and Built: Pumped Up

Delta Force Defender
Delta Force Daddy
Delta Force Die Hard

Red, White and Built

Locked, Loaded and SEALed
Alpha Bravo SEAL
Bullseye: SEAL
Point Blank SEAL
Secured by the SEAL
Bulletproof SEAL

Target: Timberline

Single Father Sheriff
Sudden Second Chance
Army Ranger Redemption
In the Arms of the Enemy

Brothers in Arms: Retribution

Under Fire
The Pregnancy Plot
Navy SEAL Spy
Secret Agent Santa

Harlequin Intrigue Noir

Toxic

Visit the Author Profile page at Harlequin.com.

CAST OF CHARACTERS

Hailey Duvall—A wealthy philanthropist, Hailey lands in the middle of a terrorist plot. When her fellow aid workers start mysteriously disappearing, she turns to a Delta Force soldier for protection and advice, even though his own agenda just might be at odds with hers.

Joe McVie—This Delta Force soldier will do anything to clear the name of Major Rex Denver, his commander who's been accused of being a traitor, and he plans to start with the lies of a wealthy socialite—but the rich girl turns out to be more than he bargained for.

Marten de Becker—An aid worker who has gone on record claiming that Major Rex Denver was behind the blast at the camp. Now he has a different story, but will he live long enough to share it?

Andrew Reese—This British journalist reporting on the Syrian refugee crisis has dropped off the face of the earth—until Hailey receives a terrifying video as a warning.

Ayala Khan—A Syrian American nurse, she's dedicated to helping her people, but her passion may have turned into a dangerous zealotry.

Naraj Siddiqi—The guide and translator on Hailey's mission has gone underground—he's either involved in the bombing of the refugee center or he's running for his life.

Major Rex Denver—Framed for working with a terrorist group, the Delta Force commander has gone AWOL and is on the run, but he knows he's onto a larger plot and can count on his squad to have his back and help clear his name.

Prologue

The boy, who'd introduced himself as Massoud, prodded his back with the old rifle as they made their way over the last of the rocks down the mountain.

The Afghan kid didn't seem to know much English beyond the words he'd used to threaten his life, or maybe his elders had ordered him to keep his mouth shut in front of strangers—especially American soldiers.

He didn't have any intention of harming the boy and hadn't taken the kid's earlier threat of bodily harm seriously. If that old Russian rifle could even shoot, Massoud barely looked big enough to hoist it and take aim. It worked well as a prop, though, giving his captor a false sense of courage.

He'd rather wind up wherever Massoud was leading him than lay waste to the kid in the mountains and be stuck making his way down by himself. He didn't lay waste to children anyway, despite what the US military believed about him.

Massoud had actually helped him navigate the terrain, which would've been difficult to do with his bum leg. Probably saved his life. Of course, he could've been saving it just to have someone else take it later.

He drew up and tripped to a stop, the boy's rifle jabbing him in the hip. He pointed to the huts with smoke rising from the center and a few goats tied up outside. He asked in Pashto, "Is this your village?"

The boy answered in English with the only words he seemed to know. "You die now, American soldier."

"Okay, okay." He held up his hands. "But you can call me Denver. I told you that. Denver."

The boy patted his own chest. "Massoud."

"I know, Massoud. Thank you for taking me down the mountain."

A flush seeped through the dirt on Massoud's grimy face as he pushed past him and greeted one of the goats with a scuff beneath its chin, his prisoner momentarily forgotten. "My home."

"Food?" Denver straightened his shoulders. He could eat one of those goats by himself—if Massoud's family didn't kill him first.

Nodding, Massoud pushed through the flap that functioned as a front door and waved him inside with the rifle.

Denver blew out a breath and shrugged his own weapon off his back. He leaned it against the side of the hut, leaving his sidearm strapped to his thigh. Massoud's family had to realize that if he hadn't used his weapons to kill their son, he didn't plan to use them against the other family members, either.

He ducked inside the dark, smoky room, and his eyes watered. A pot of something savory hung over a fire, bubbling with a thick concoction that made his stomach growl.

A small woman hunched over the fire, stirring the contents of the cauldron without looking up from her task.

Massoud rattled off something in Pashto, too fast for Denver to catch all the words except *American*, but whatever he said had an instantaneous effect on the woman cooking.

She whirled around, the spoon in her hand dripping hot liquid onto the dirt floor. She swung the spoon at Massoud, the words tumbling from her lips and droplets flying from the utensil. When she stopped to take a breath, she scuttled into another room—probably the only other room in the structure.

Massoud pushed Denver in the direction of the flap at the front, and he stepped outside again, breathing deeply of the fresh air. The woman didn't seem too happy to see him, but at least nobody had shot him between the eyes…yet.

Massoud put two fingers in his mouth and whistled. Less than a minute later, a middle-aged man appeared at the door of another hut. He squinted at Massoud and his…guest and then jerked back. He said something over his shoulder and strode forward.

When he was halfway to Massoud, the boy ran to him, waving his arms and pointing back to Denver.

The man put his hand on Massoud's shoulder and

walked him slowly back to Denver. He dipped his head in Denver's direction and spoke in slow, careful English. "I am Massoud's father, Rafi."

"Major Rex Denver, United States Army."

The man nodded. "I know who you are. The American traitor…and I know why you're here."

Chapter One

The chill bit into Hailey's cheeks as she slid from the taxi. She hunched into her coat, crushing her ticket to Alcatraz in her pocket. Even on a chilly January evening, you needed to get a ticket in advance for the ferry to Alcatraz.

If Marten wanted to hit the tourist spots of the city, she would've been happy to oblige and they could've had this meeting over lunch instead of trying to talk on a crowded, windblown ferry. But Marten never made anything easy.

He'd even insisted that she board the ferry without him and wait for him on the boat—as if he didn't want to be seen with her. She could never tell if Marten's penchant for secrecy stemmed from reality or a yearning to play spy.

As Hailey lined up for the day's last ferry to Alcatraz, she pressed a hand against her midsection—and it had nothing to do with seasickness.

Marten *had* been secretive. Had asked her not to mention their meeting to anyone. Had refused to come to her place in Pacific Heights, and now he didn't even want to be seen boarding the ferry with her.

His fear couldn't have anything to do with what happened in Syria, could it? The CIA and the Department of Defense had already debriefed them about the incident and released them—told them to go home. *Ordered* them to go home.

She checked her phone cupped in her palm. Marten hadn't responded to her previous text letting him know she was on her way. She zipped off another one giving him her current status.

The line of people started shuffling forward, and Hailey moved with them. She handed over her ticket and walked onto the ferry, cranking her head back to see if she could catch a glimpse of Marten's black porkpie hat—his signature fashion accessory. He'd even worn it in Syria at the refugee camp, to the delight of all the children there.

Hailey gulped back the lump of tears lodged in her throat.

The faces of the people in the crowd merged behind her and she stumbled, grabbing on to a handrail. Once on the ferry, she walked up two flights of steps to the third level to get a better view of the rest of the tourists pouring onto the boat.

When she reached the top level, she rested her back against the railing and scanned the San Francisco skyline, which stood in stark relief against the dark blue sky. Winter in the city could be crisp and clear and achingly beautiful—too bad she had to waste this moment on Marten and one of his silly games.

The ferry captain made a few announcements as the boat chugged away from the dock. Had Marten even boarded? She glanced at her phone again. Was he going to give her a meeting place or make her wander around the boat looking for him?

The ferry plowed forward, carving its way through the choppy water of the bay. Hailey spotted a man in a black hat like Marten's on the second level.

Leaning over, she waved to get his attention, but he seemed to be focused on something in front of him. Wasn't Marten even looking for her? Why didn't he just respond to her texts? Typical Marten.

"Excuse me." She squeezed past a bunch of people near the stairs and headed down to the deck below, the heels of her boots clanging on the metal steps. Not the most practical boating shoes, but she didn't plan to hoist a sail or anything.

She followed the path she had seen Marten taking to the front of the ferry as it nosed its way to Alcatraz. Standing on her tiptoes, she gazed at the people milling around the deck, phones out, taking pictures of the shore, Coit Tower gleaming in the distance, and then swinging around and taking pictures of Angel Island and the fast-approaching prison on Alcatraz.

She huffed out a breath of annoyance through her nose. No sight of Marten. What kind of game was he playing with her? There had always been whispers about Marten posing as a relief worker to spy—rumors he'd done nothing to squelch. She'd always brushed them off before, but his actions today sure hinted at covert activity.

Up ahead, a commotion broke out along the railing of the boat. A few people screamed, and a man yelled.

As Hailey drew closer, her heart picking up speed, she heard a man shout, "Man overboard. Man overboard."

A sickening dread punched her in the gut. She pushed her way toward the crowd of people hanging over the side of the ferry, staring at the rough water churning beneath the boat.

As Hailey drew closer to the mayhem, she spotted a black hat on the deck. Her heart stuttered and she lunged forward to retrieve the hat, only to be blocked by a crew member.

With his arm barring her progress, the crew member shouted, "Back up. Everyone back away from this area of the ferry."

The boat cut its speed and started making a wide turn. The people on the upper deck and those inside who didn't know what had happened mumbled in unison, creating a howl that rolled across the bay.

More crew members fanned out on the deck and began herding people to the other side of the boat.

An announcement boomed on the loudspeaker. "Anyone who witnessed the man going over or who has any information about him or the incident, gather inside at the bar."

So, someone *had* gone into the water. Hailey secured the scarf tighter around her neck. Did she have any information? Was that Marten's hat?

She pulled out her phone and texted him again.

A coast guard boat joined them within minutes, and the ferry began to head back to the pier, but they weren't going to let anyone off the boat just yet. A deadly calm and order fell over the ferry as people began to form knots, discussing the incident and complaining about their interrupted trip.

Hailey decided to join the group by the bar. Marten hadn't texted her back yet. Listening to snatches of conversations, it seemed as if nobody had actually witnessed the man falling overboard. A few claimed to have seen a man in the water, but no groups were missing anyone from their party—nobody but her.

She shuffled up to a crew member behind the bar, who raised his eyebrows. "Did you see something?"

"No, but…" Hailey bit her lip. How stupid did her story sound?

The crew member tapped his pen on the pad of paper beneath his arm. "Yes?"

"I—I was supposed to meet someone on board, and I thought I saw him wearing that black hat. He did wear a hat like that."

"What hat?"

"There was a black hat on the deck where the man went over."

He drew his brows together. "I don't know anything about a hat. Go on. You were meeting him on the ferry?"

Hailey flipped one end of her scarf over her shoulder. "He indicated that he was going to be running late and might miss the ferry, so he told me to go ahead and board without him."

"The man's name?"

"Marten de Becker."

He scribbled Marten's name beneath several other notes he'd already taken. "I'm going to radio his name back to the office on the pier so we can check out his ticket and if he boarded the ferry."

Hailey nodded and stepped to the side, folding her hands around the cup of coffee that the crew members had handed out earlier. It couldn't be Marten. Why would Marten jump off a ferry when they had a meeting planned?

Several minutes later, the man turned back toward her. "There was no Marten de Becker who bought a ticket or boarded the ferry. Sounds like you and your friend got your dates or times mixed up."

Hailey's shoulders slumped, warm relief flooding her body. "Nobody is missing yet?"

"The office is narrowing down the names, but we won't release anything until the next of kin is notified."

"It's horrible. Do you have cameras on that area of the ferry?"

"No cameras on the boat, but we do have them back at the loading area."

After several more minutes, people began disembarking, and the captain announced that another ferry would be there to meet them if any passengers wanted to return to Alcatraz and continue their trip.

Hailey didn't have any reason to return to Alcatraz. She'd been there a hundred times. How could people carry on with their plans with the lights from the coast guard boats still illuminating the bay searching for someone?

As her boots clattered over the gangplank, Hailey checked her phone for a text response from Marten, but he hadn't replied. He'd be sorry he missed all the excitement. Marten loved excitement. Her gaze tracked back to the bay and the coast guard boats now in the distance. A chill touched her spine, as if she were out there struggling in the cold water.

Hailey wandered away from the ferry terminal, her head bent over her phone, pulling up a car app. As her finger hovered over the display to accept a ride, a text came through.

She caught her breath when she saw Marten's name. She tapped the message and read aloud, "'Changed my mind.'"

"What?" She clenched her teeth from screaming. After all that trouble and…worry, and he changed his mind about the meeting?

She responded, I thought you were here. Where are you now and why playing games? Call me.

Her gaze burned a hole in her phone as she waited for Marten's response. Someone bumped her elbow and she glanced up.

"Sorry." A woman held up her hand. "Were you on that ferry to Alcatraz?"

"I was."

"What happened? I heard someone went over-board."

"That's what they told us, but nobody seems to be missing anyone. I guess they're checking tickets now and the coast guard is still searching the bay."

The woman hunched her shoulders. "Is that going to be a thing now? Instead of jumping from the bridge, they're going to jump from the ferry?"

"Jump?" Hailey massaged the back of her neck.

"Nobody just falls off the Alcatraz ferry." The woman waved at a man approaching and glanced over her shoulder. "Have a nice night."

Suicide? Who would commit suicide by jumping off the ferry to Alcatraz? Especially Marten.

Hailey shook her head and peered at her phone. She input a row of question marks for the silent Marten.

"Now what?" She crossed her arms and scanned the crowd of tourists streaming along the Embarcadero on their way to and from Fisherman's Wharf and Pier 39 with all its shops and restaurants.

Food. Marten had insisted on the night tour to Alcatraz, and now her stomach was growling. She'd head down to Fisherman's Wharf with the rest of the tourists and pick up some seafood from the sidewalk stands.

Cranking her head over her shoulder, she took a last look at the ferry terminal. Had the man who'd gone overboard been wearing a black hat…like Marten's? Where had the hat gone?

But Marten had never boarded the ferry. He'd never even bought a ticket.

She looked at her phone again. Why wouldn't he answer her? He'd better be prepared for questions when they got together, because she had a ton.

She shoved the phone in her pocket and joined the hordes on the sidewalk. She wove her way through the tourists as they stopped to watch the performers along the street.

When she reached the seafood stands on the sidewalk, she jostled for position, elbowing with the best of them. She leaned forward and ordered some clam chowder in a sourdough bread bowl.

Clutching her plate with the bowl of steaming chowder perched on top of it, she wormed her way back to the sidewalk and walked toward a set of wooden steps that led down to the part of the wharf with the maritime museum and the submarine, both closed at this time of night and affording a little calm from the chaos on the sidewalk above. She'd try giving Marten a call.

When she was about halfway down the steps, someone came up behind her and grabbed her arm. Her heart slammed against her chest, and her dinner began tipping to the side.

The man steadied her plate and whispered in her ear, "Act naturally. Someone's following you—the same person who murdered Marten de Becker."

Chapter Two

Hailey Duvall's slim hand formed a fist, and he clenched his jaw, bracing for a punch to his face.

A shadow passed over them from the top of the stairs, and Joe threw his head back and laughed. Pretending he and Hailey were old friends, he said to her, "I told you to get me some food. I'll take one of these."

A crease formed between Hailey's delicate eyebrows, and her nostrils flared. Her gaze dropped to the bread bowl, steam rising from the chowder. The corner of her eye twitched.

Was she going to toss it at him?

Joe's muscles ached from the smile plastered onto his face. "Can we go back upstairs where it's populated and talk this through?"

"Who are you?" She released the plate they both held with a jerk, and the soup spilled over the edge of the hollowed-out sourdough and ran down the side of the bread bowl.

"My name is Joe McVie. I'm a captain with the US Army, Delta Force."

She blinked her long, dark lashes rapidly, and her chest rose and fell.

That meant something to her. Good.

"I want to talk to you about Marten de Becker and what just happened on the ferry to Alcatraz."

"H-he never made it onto the ferry." She pulled her phone out of her pocket and held it up, her hand trembling. "I got a text from him after the accident. Were you on the ferry?"

"I followed Marten onto the ferry. He was wearing a black hat with a black-and-white-checkered band around it. He never came off that ferry—at least he didn't walk off."

She stepped back from him and twisted her head to the side to take in the mostly empty walkway along where the submarine was docked. Her tongue darted from her mouth and swept across her bottom lip.

Joe took a step up. "Let's go where it's crowded. Where you'll feel safer. I'm not here to scare you."

She tipped her firm chin toward the stairs, not looking afraid in the least. "You first."

Holding the plate with two hands, Joe climbed the stairs and stood to the side to wait for Hailey to pass at the top. "I wasn't kidding about the food. I'm hungry, and this smells great."

She pointed to one of the fish stands on the street. "I got it there. You take mine and find a table. I'll get another and join you...unless I decide to make my escape. And if I do and you try to follow me, I'll call the cops so fast your...red head will spin."

Joe let out a breath on a smile. "You're not my captive, but I think you're gonna want to hear what I have to say. I'll grab a seat on the patio behind us."

Hailey spun away from him and dived into the mob of people clustered around the stand.

If she took off and melted into the crowd, he wouldn't blame her. But something in her sparkling eyes told him the news about de Becker didn't surprise her. Whether or not she believed his claim about someone tailing her just now remained to be seen.

He kept his gaze pinned on her while she ordered another bowl of chowder. Hailey Duvall would stand out in any crowd—tall, dark and beautiful. She wore her wealth with an easy grace. Even a philistine like him could spot the expensive clothes, the designer leather bag slung casually over one shoulder, the perfect hair and makeup that came only from the best products and pampering.

What the hell had she been doing in Syria?

She got her food and ducked between the tourists. Halfway back to the tables on the patio, her step faltered. Then she met his eyes, squared her shoulders and continued her approach.

Maybe she figured if he were going to harm her, he'd have done it downstairs without such a big audience. Maybe she wanted to find out what had happened to de Becker and why.

He could deliver on that for sure.

As she drew within a few feet of the table, Joe jumped

up from his metal chair and pulled one out for her, wiping the seat with a napkin. "You never know about these seagulls out here."

"Thanks." She sat down, placing the plate with the bread bowl in front of her. "Where's the man who was following me? Or was that just a ruse to play the good guy and then hit me with your crazy theory about Marten?"

"It's not a theory, and you know it, Hailey."

Her eyes widened. "How do you know my name? Were you part of the military that came to the refugee center…after?"

"No, but I know all about the refugee camp and what happened there."

She covered her eyes with one hand, the big diamond on one finger flashing in the night. "It was horrible, and we were responsible."

"No, you weren't—and neither was Major Denver."

She split her fingers and peeked at him through the space. "That's not what Marten said."

"Was de Becker the only one of your group who identified Denver at that meeting?"

"Meeting?" She picked up her spoon and began stirring her soup as her mouth tightened. "That was no meeting. The other aid workers, our guide and I were all kidnapped. Then they planted a bomb in our car and sent us back to the refugee center—to kill people."

"Sorry, I used the wrong word." He touched the back of her smooth hand with his finger—at least that diamond graced her right hand and not her left, not that her marital status meant anything to him one way or the other. "That must've been terrible for all of you."

"Worse for the people who died in the bomb blast." Hunching her shoulders, she blew on a spoonful of chowder. "So, you know all about me and that... incident. Are you representing the US Army, reaching out to me in some official capacity?"

"Official?" He broke off a piece of bread from the side of the bowl. "Nah."

"What do you know about Marten de Becker?" She puckered her lips and blew on a spoonful of soup before sipping it.

Dragging his gaze away from her pouting lips, he said, "I know he had a change of heart about who exactly kidnapped your group."

"Were you following him?"

"Yes." He dragged the piece of sourdough through the creamy chowder and popped it in his mouth. "I knew he was here to see you. I've been keeping tabs on you, too. All of you."

"You've been following me?" Her eyebrows snapped over her nose.

He didn't have to follow Hailey Duvall to know who she was—heir, along with her brother, to a fortune made in real estate; philanthropist; do-gooder and blessed with a natural beauty that took his breath away. That last part he'd just discovered tonight.

All the magazine pictures and video couldn't do justice to the vitality that radiated from her slender body and shone in her eyes. Hailey wouldn't be one to play tennis and lunch with other socialites. She had an energy about her that made you think she was ready to jump out of her seat and do something important.

"Following you? Not like I was following de Becker. He's the one who fingered Denver."

"You're sure he got on that ferry?" She tucked a lock of dark, glossy hair behind her ear.

"I tracked him from his hotel. I was following the man in the black hat. That man never got off the boat."

She toyed with her spoon. "I gave his name to a crew member and he phoned it in. Marten de Becker never bought a ticket tonight."

"He must've bought it under a different name." Joe shrugged. He had his own suspicions about de Becker.

"I told you before, he texted me after the accident on the ferry. Wrote that he changed his mind."

"Someone has his phone. Probably took it before he pushed Marten overboard."

Hailey dropped her plastic spoon, and it fell on the ground. "Why would someone kill Marten? Why are you keeping track of us?"

"It all has to do with that kidnapping and what you saw and heard. It has to do with Major Rex Denver." He pointed to her spoon on the ground. "Do you want another?"

"I've lost my appetite."

"Tell me, Hailey. Why did de Becker want to meet you tonight? And why on a ferry to Alcatraz?"

"I have no idea. I haven't seen him since the bombing at the refugee camp. He called me out of the blue yesterday. I invited him to dinner, but he insisted on meeting on the ferry."

"Did he give you any hints about what he wanted?"

"Told me to keep quiet about him and our meeting." She pushed away her plate and folded her hands on the metal table. "He sounded…strange, secretive. All my instincts told me not to meet him—at least not the way he wanted."

"Do you always ignore your instincts?"

She crumpled her napkin in her fist and slammed it on the table. "If you're implying I had any inkling those…terrorists planted a bomb underneath the car for our trip back to the refugee center, you couldn't be more wrong. None of us believed those men waylaid us for that purpose."

"I'm not suggesting that." He held up his hands. "Why would you think they wanted to send a bomb into the refugee camp? But what *did* you think they wanted when they kidnapped you?"

Her dark eyes flashed, and their fire sent a thrill down his spine. The cool, calm and collected princess had a dangerous side.

He spoke in a soothing tone, wary of setting her off. "I just want to know what you thought, what you all thought. I want to know who first suggested the American with your captors was Major Rex Denver."

She kept hold of the napkin and began shredding pieces from it. "We were coming back to the refugee camp from a supply center in Pakistan. There were five of us—me, Marten, Andrew Reese, the British journalist, Ayala Khan, who's one of the nurses at the center, and our guide and translator, Naraj Siddiqi."

Joe had his doubts about Siddiqi, but he'd keep those to himself right now. "How'd they capture you?"

"Familiar story." She shrugged. "A couple of guys ran our car off the road. They had bigger weapons than our guide and forced us into the back of their truck. They blindfolded us and took us to some bombed-out buildings."

"You couldn't see. How'd you know about the buildings?"

"I could just tell—the dust, the silence, the rubble. While they led us along, they had to keep telling us to step up, step to the side. Even with the warnings, I tripped and stumbled a hundred times. I could tell we were in some bombed-out ghost of a neighborhood."

"Did they mistreat you?" His jaw hardened at the thought of Hailey in the hands of the insurgents in that area.

"No. Offered us tea, but kept us blindfolded."

"And that's when you heard the American? Did he speak to you?"

"We just heard his voice a few times. He spoke French to one of the kidnappers. I could tell he was American from his accent." A flush stained her cheeks. "I—I speak French fluently."

Of course she did. Probably learned it at one of those fancy boarding schools.

Joe ripped off a side of the bread bowl. "The American didn't speak Syrian?"

"No."

Joe crumbled the bread in the remains of his soup.

Hailey hunched forward. "Why? What does that mean?"

"Denver speaks several languages, including Syrian. If he were there, why wouldn't he converse in that language instead of some awful French?"

"I didn't say his French was awful." She tossed her mangled napkin on the table beside her plate. "Maybe that's exactly why he didn't speak Syrian. How many Americans know that language? Maybe he didn't want to give himself away."

Joe snorted. "Major Denver wasn't there. No way. He wouldn't send a bomb into a refugee center targeting helpless people—women and children. No way."

"So that's what this is all about. You, here, following de Becker around. Did the army send you? Delta Force?"

"I'm here on my own, on leave. The US Army has no idea I'm following up on this and it wouldn't be appreciated or condoned...but I don't give a damn about that."

"What makes you so sure Denver didn't go rogue? Didn't he go AWOL?"

"I know him. I'm a good judge of character. He went AWOL because he realized he was being set up. Whoever set him up had already killed an Army Ranger and tried to kill one of our Delta Force team members. The army tried to pin it all on Denver, but that team member, Asher Knight, got his memories back and insisted that he, the Army Ranger and Denver were all set up at that meeting."

"You think our kidnapping is another plot to implicate Major Denver?"

"That's exactly what I think. Who first told you about Denver? Wasn't de Becker the one who initially ID'd Denver as being present at that…gathering before the bomb went off in the refugee camp?"

"It was Marten. I can't even remember how that all came about. I was devastated, in shock after the explosion. They made us all leave the camp—the country—after that." Her voice wavered.

"Did anyone question you?" Joe resisted the urge to take her hand.

"Of course." As if reading his mind, she put her hand in her pocket. "We were questioned there, and people from the Department of Defense came out here to San Francisco to question me and then the FBI sent a couple of agents for good measure. We went through the wringer."

"Did they ask you about Denver and whether or not you could ID him? I know de Becker said that his blindfold had slipped and he saw the American. When they showed him Denver's picture, he picked him out."

"I know that." She straightened out her scarf and smoothed it against the front of her jacket. "My blindfold was secure and I never saw a thing, never saw any of my captors."

Joe slumped in his chair. "So, you never claimed that Denver was there."

"I said I didn't *see* my captors." She held up one finger, her perfectly polished fingernail catching the light from the streetlamp next to their table, making it look like a magic wand. "I did hear them."

"And?" He ran a tongue around his dry mouth.

"And in addition to hearing an American speaking French, I heard someone call someone else Denver."

Joe sank his head in his hands, his fingers digging into his scalp. "No."

"I'm sorry. I did hear that, and I reported it to the military investigators."

"If the major wanted to keep his presence there a secret, why would the others be throwing around his name? That makes no sense."

"I agree, unless someone slipped up." She touched his sleeve. "You still haven't told me why someone would want to kill Marten."

"Because of all this." He swept his arm to the side, encompassing the bay. "De Becker was making noises about taking back his eyewitness statement placing Denver in Syria outside that refugee camp."

"Why is that a problem? Doesn't the army want the truth? Doesn't the CIA?"

"They may want the truth, but there are factions in some high places that want to perpetuate this lie about Major Denver. We just don't know why."

"We?"

"A couple of my Delta Force team members have already uncovered some discrepancies in these stories swirling around Denver. Things are not adding up."

"These highly placed factions are willing to commit murder to further their narrative?" Hailey put a hand to her throat. "To follow around innocent citizens?"

"Your meeting with de Becker never happened. You don't know why he wanted to talk to you." Joe pinched the bridge of his nose between his thumb and forefinger. "If anyone ever follows up with you, tell them you heard the name Denver used for one of your kidnappers and leave it at that."

It was not the speech he'd planned to deliver to Hailey Duvall. He'd wanted her to step forward and question the investigators' insistence that the major was there, that it was ludicrous to believe they'd use his real name under those circumstances. But after meeting and talking with Hailey, all he wanted to do was protect her. Keep her away from this madness.

She'd already been through enough. Her car had delivered a bomb inside a refugee center filled with innocents. Even though it wasn't her fault, she'd have to carry that with her. And he could tell—this would weigh on her.

Why else would an über-rich woman spend her time and money to help people halfway across the world? Put herself in danger to do so? When he'd started this journey, he thought Hailey was a naive do-gooder. Now he felt humbled in the presence of her selflessness.

She tapped her fingers on the table. "If I stick to that story, how are you going to prove Denver wasn't responsible for the bombing of the refugee camp?"

"I'll prove it another way." He swept up his plate with its collapsing bread bowl. "But I'd like to see you home, if that's okay."

Her gaze shifted to the sidewalk, still jammed with tourists. "Do you think I'm in danger?"

He lifted one shoulder. "That guy was probably just following you to see if you'd go to the police with any suspicions about the man who went overboard. If they do have de Becker's phone, maybe you can just play it cool and text him as if he blew off your date."

"I already did text him—and that was no date." She plowed her fingers through her hair. "If Marten was murdered, do you think I can sit back and pretend this night never happened? If it turns out that was Marten, I'm going to go to the police *and* the FBI and tell them about our planned meeting and the texts I received from his phone after his death."

"Not sure that would be wise at this point, Hailey."

"Wise?" Her eyes grew round. "It's what's right. It's justice."

Uneasiness gnawed at his gut. Did he really think Hailey would drop this after all she'd gone through? He should've just made sure she came to no harm tonight. He never should've intervened and approached her. A woman like Hailey spelled danger for him ten different ways.

The truth smacked him in the face, and he swallowed. Once he'd gotten an eyeful of Hailey, he felt compelled to make a move. How else was he gonna meet a woman like this? They didn't travel in the same circles...and that poor boy from South Boston still desperately yearned to be accepted by those women out of his reach—the one that got away. *Pathetic bastard.*

Hailey stood up suddenly. "You can see me home if you like. I was going to call an online car before I got the bright idea that I needed something to eat down here."

"And you never even ate." He pointed to the chowder, cold and soaking into its bowl.

"Like I said, lost my appetite."

As she strolled toward the curb, bent over her phone, Joe grabbed their trash and dumped it in the nearest can.

She held up her cell as he approached her. "I told him to meet us up the street a little to avoid the traffic around here."

"Is Pacific Heights close?"

Sliding a glance to the side, she said, "You really did your research, didn't you? You even know where I live."

"C'mon, Hailey. It's not exactly hard to find out where you live. You're kinda all over San Francisco society news."

"Sometimes this can really seem like a small town." She bumped his elbow with her own. "Let's cross."

He didn't presume to take her arm as they crossed the street, but he wanted to. Everyone she came in contact with must feel that way about her—drawn to her vitality and warmth. He was simply one of many who swarmed around her, wanting to be close.

The phone in her hand rang, and she brought it to her face. "Yeah, right in front of the T-shirt shop. I see you—black Nissan."

As the black car pulled up to the curb, Joe shot forward and opened the door for Hailey.

She slid into the back seat, and he followed.

Hunching forward, she asked, "Do you need directions?"

"I have it on my GPS. Pacific Avenue in Pacific Heights, right?"

"That's it." She settled back and closed her eyes. "When do you think we'll find out about Marten?"

"If he didn't buy the ticket under his own name and they don't—" Joe glanced at the rearview mirror "—find the body, it could take a while. If he washes up somewhere and they can get fingerprints, they'll eventually ID him."

"He's Dutch, you know, a Dutch citizen, and they'll ID him a lot faster when I step forward and report him missing."

Joe put a finger to his lips. He was beginning to understand that once Hailey got her teeth into something, she became a pit bull.

A totally gorgeous pit bull with really nice teeth.

Several minutes later, Hailey tapped the back of the driver's seat. "It's the one on the left. You can pull over here."

The driver whistled as he stopped his car. "That must be a great view during the day. Not bad at night, either."

"It is. Thanks." Hailey turned to Joe. "Do you want to keep the car for wherever you're going next?"

"You're not getting rid of me that easily. I'll see you to the front door."

The driver adjusted the rearview mirror. "I can wait here, but you'll have to call me up again on the app."

"I'll do it when we get up to the house. If you get another fare, take it."

Hailey slid from the car and Joe followed her out and trailed after her as she strode across the street.

His jaw dropped slightly when he got a load of the house looming in front of him. The huge white house, gleaming in the night, had a fountain and a garden in front and what looked like a four-car garage on the lower level. Being in San Francisco, and Pacific Heights in particular, they had to walk up some steps to get to the front door.

"I'm sure it's okay. I even have security cameras." She pointed to the eaves of the house as she charged ahead of him. Then she tripped to a stop and gasped.

His hand shot out to grab her arm, and she spun in his grasp, almost falling into his arms from the step above.

"Are you all right?"

She shook her head and stepped to the side—revealing a black hat with a checkered band resting on her welcome mat.

Some welcome.

Chapter Three

Hailey's knees wobbled and she took an unsteady step down—away from Marten's hat—even though it put her chest to chest with Joe.

His arm curled around her back, and she didn't even jerk away. She needed support right now —and this solid hunk of man fit the bill.

"It's Marten's, isn't it? That's the hat I was following all day until I trailed him to the ferry to Alcatraz. Any doubts now?"

Even Joe's voice, low and rumbling, represented safety.

"How did it end up here? It was on the deck after… he went overboard. Wouldn't the crew have picked it up? Why would they allow some random person to grab the hat of the guy who'd just taken a dive off the boat?"

"There was mass confusion in the moments after the other passengers reported that a man had gone into the water. Anyone could've snatched up the hat."

Someone honked a horn, and Hailey jumped, putting her even closer to Joe and his warm presence.

He squeezed her waist. "It's the driver. I'll tell him not to wait. He'll just think I got lucky."

With her head to one side, Hailey watched Joe jog down the steps to the sidewalk. Got lucky? Was that what he was hoping for? Was that what *she* was hoping for?

As he returned to the porch, Hailey leaned over the hat, giving it a wide berth, and unlocked her front door. She pushed it open and jerked her thumb up to the roof. "I'm going to get a look at exactly who left the hat when I check my security footage, and then I'm going to call the police."

"You're going to call the police on someone for leaving a hat on your doorstep?" Joe crouched down and picked up the hat by its brim. "Maybe the SFPD jumps when someone from Pacific Heights calls, but I doubt this offense would be high on their agenda."

"The hat of someone who was pushed off an Alcatraz ferry?"

"Nobody said he was pushed. There were no witnesses. He could've fallen. Jumped. There's no…body yet."

She turned toward him, still not sure whether or not she was inviting him inside. "Why'd they do it? Why leave Marten's hat here?"

"As a warning? I don't know." He tipped the hat at her. "Let's take a look at that security footage."

He'd made the decision for her, invited himself in... and she didn't mind one bit.

She widened the door and stepped back, holding her breath as Joe crossed the threshold into the foyer. The opulence of the house could make people dizzy—or make them salivate. She'd seen both reactions from men she'd ushered inside—and either way, it had ended badly for her and not too great for them, either.

Joe didn't even blink an eyelash as he placed the hat on a bench in the entryway and touched her arm. "Are you sure you're okay? You look pale. Maybe you should sit down before chasing after that footage."

"I'm fine, thanks." She scooped up a remote control by the door and clicked a few buttons, turning on the lights in the kitchen. "I can bring up the security cam on my laptop."

Her heels tapped on the polished hardwood floor as she walked toward the kitchen, Joe dogging her steps as if he feared she'd keel over in a faint. Despite their cushy surroundings, Joe had to realize she was made of stronger stuff than that, although she didn't know why she cared what Joe McVie thought.

She flipped up the lid on her laptop and tapped the keyboard to wake it up. Her fingers hovered over the keys as Joe leaned over her shoulder.

She flicked her fingers at him. "I'm going to enter my password now."

"Oh, sorry." He circled around until his back was facing her.

Typing in her password, she asked, "Do you want something to drink? I have beer and some white wine in the fridge."

"Just some water, please."

"Bottles are in the refrigerator." She drummed her thumbs on the base of the computer. "I haven't looked at this in a while."

"I can help you, if you need it." Joe held up a water bottle. "Do you want one?"

"No, thanks, but you can pour me a glass of that chardonnay that's open. Glass in the cupboard to your right."

While Joe clinked through the glasses and poured her wine, she navigated to the security program and launched the footage.

"Your wine." Joe clicked the glass on the counter next to the computer and took up his previous position behind her, looking over her shoulder. He jabbed his finger at the screen. "You can get to the date there. Today's date is the default."

"I've got it. Thanks for the wine." She picked up the glass and raised it, tapping it against his plastic water bottle. "Here's to success."

He repeated, "Success."

She sipped her wine as she double clicked today's date and then scrolled through the day. "There's my mail person. I don't think *she* left it."

"You can jump to four o'clock. It had to be after that time."

"I'm getting there." Hailey pursed her lips. She

never did meet a man who wasn't bossy. Then she sucked in a breath. "There he is. He left the hat just over an hour ago."

Joe hunched forward, his warm breath tickling her ear. "Damn. Looks like he knew he could be on camera."

Hailey froze the video and traced her finger around the black-clad figure with the ski mask pulled down over his face. "Not very helpful, is it? He's even wearing gloves, so the police wouldn't be able to pick up any fingerprints."

"I can't even tell if it's the same person who was following you on the wharf. He probably would've had enough time to beat us here." Joe blew out a breath and her hair stirred against her cheek. "You're still thinking about calling the cops? Where I come from, the cops would barely move for a dead body on your porch. A hat? They'd laugh in your face."

She twisted her head over her shoulder. "Where do you come from?"

"South side of Boston, although it's been a while since I've been back."

"Rough area?"

"You could say that." He leveled his finger at the display. "Let's see what else he does."

She restarted the video and watched the disguised man—person—drop the hat on the porch, turn, jog down the steps and hit the sidewalk. "Nothing."

"You don't have a camera pointing at the street?"

"Not anymore. It broke and I never got around to

fixing it. I doubt this guy would be dumb enough to drive up to the front of the house, anyway."

"You're probably right." Joe slammed his bottle on the counter next to her glass. "They're warning you to keep your mouth shut about Marten and about the abduction in Syria—and you're gonna do it."

She hooked her heels on the bar beneath the stool and snapped the laptop closed on the frozen image of Marten's hat on her porch. "What about Major Denver?"

"We'll figure it out. Don't worry about it. You reported what you heard from your captors, and you told the truth. That's all anyone can ask. That's all I can ask."

"And Marten?"

"He got mixed up in something he should've left alone."

"Wasn't he just telling the truth?"

"Was he?" Joe rubbed a hand across the sexy burnished-gold stubble on his jaw. "I don't believe Marten did tell the truth. Someone got to him, and he lied to promote the Denver narrative. Who knows? Maybe he was paid off. Then he stopped playing the game, and that's when he got into trouble."

Hailey traced a finger around the rim of her wineglass. "That sounds like Marten."

"Does it?"

"Marten was a gambler. Last I heard, he was in debt. I wouldn't put it past him to lie in exchange for money."

"What was a guy like that doing aiding refugees?"

"He liked excitement." She shrugged. "I'm not sure what he was doing in Syria, but I had my suspicions that he'd worked as a mercenary for the Kurds before joining us."

"What about the others? Ayala? The journalist? Your guide, Siddiqi?"

"Ayala's a nurse from Florida. She's already back at the camp. Andrew is back in England writing other stories. Naraj is probably back at work. He's a freelancer for hire. He escorts crazy Westerners around for a price."

Joe pinched his chin and stared over her head. "Convenient."

"Ah, no." She waved her hand in front of his face to break his gaze. "Naraj didn't betray us."

"How'd that group of thugs know you'd be on the road at that particular time?"

"We weren't far from the refugee camp when they took us. They were probably lying in wait for the first opportunity."

"But *your* car, the one eventually heading back to the camp. That explosion derailed the peace negotiations between the Syrian government and the rebels—each blaming each other and getting maximum propaganda points out of the carnage."

"I know." Hailey put a hand over her aching heart.

"You had no way of knowing your kidnappers were going to plant that bomb on your car." He shoved her wineglass toward her, and the golden liquid inside sloshed and sparkled.

Curling two fingers around the stem of the glass, she said, "It's still hard not to feel responsible. We brought that death and destruction into the camp."

"I'm sorry. It's nasty business out there."

Joe placed two fingers on the base of her glass, brushing her hand and causing butterflies to flutter in her stomach.

Must be the emotions of the day that had her so susceptible to this Delta Force soldier on a mission. It couldn't be his dark russet hair and rough-around-the-edges manner. That type hadn't appealed to her since her teen years, when she'd been trying to get her father's attention. It hadn't worked anyway, and the guys ended up being as untrustworthy as the rich boys—just in a different way.

She blinked. "Thanks. I don't think Naraj betrayed us, though."

"Are you safe in this house?" Joe downed the rest of his water and screwed the lid back on the bottle.

He was leaving her.

"Yes, of course. In addition to the security cameras, there's an alarm system."

"I didn't see you set one."

"I didn't. I don't always arm it."

"Why not?" He pushed off the stool and, spreading his arms, did a slow turn around the room. "There's some artwork on that wall over there that could feed a family of five for life."

Heat surged into her cheeks. So he'd only pretended not to notice the luxury of the house. "This is my father's house."

"And you don't care if your father loses his assets?" His brows shot up to his hairline.

"Considering how he amassed his fortune?" She tossed her head, sweeping her hair from her shoulder. "Not really."

"He's a real-estate mogul, not a drug dealer, right?"

"Forget it." She didn't want to go into a petulant first-world rant about her father's wealth in front of Joe. "I will definitely set the alarm system tonight."

"Good, because you're the most valuable thing in this whole house."

And just like that, her heart flip-flopped, but not from fear.

"Do you think I might actually be in danger?" She took a swig of her wine.

"I think you'll be fine if you stick to your original story and don't make waves about Marten."

"That seems—" she swirled the last of the liquid in her glass "—wrong."

"You can't do anything for Marten now, Hailey. Stay on script. Any chance your father is coming home anytime soon?"

"He's in New York with his wife. She prefers it there."

"And your brother?"

Hailey swallowed. Joe really knew her entire family history. "My brother, Win, will be wherever our father is, playing lapdog."

"Speaking of dogs, you don't have a German shepherd hiding out somewhere, do you?" Joe leaned forward as if to peek under the sofa in the next room.

"Mel, my stepmother, can't stand animals. As soon as my cat died, she declared a moratorium on pets in this house."

"Don't you have a house of your own?"

"No. I gave up my apartment near the Haight when I went to Syria. When I came back home, my father asked me to live in and watch his place."

"You could do a lot worse." He crushed the water bottle with one hand. "As long as you're here and as long as there's an alarm system, use it."

"I will now." She held up her phone. "Do you want me to call you a car? Where are you staying, anyway?"

"Hotel back by Fisherman's Wharf." He pulled a wallet out of his pocket. "I'll pay you back for the car."

"Don't worry about it. It'll only be a few bucks." At least Joe didn't assume Miss Moneybags would be picking up the tab for everything.

He waved a twenty in the air before slipping it beneath her wineglass. "Take it for the transportation and the dinner."

"The dinner?"

"I stole your chowder and then ruined your appetite."

"You did do that." She tapped her phone to accept a driver in the vicinity. "Your car's on its way, a white Prius."

"Thanks, Hailey, and I'm sorry I messed up your evening." He held out his hand. "It was nice meeting you."

She took his hand, and it enveloped hers in a warm clasp. "I appreciate what you did tonight—I mean, ensuring my safety. What's next for you?"

"I'll continue looking into the claim that Denver was part of the group that planted the bomb on your car." He flipped up the collar of his jacket. "I might track down the journalist who was with you."

"I told you, Andrew Reese is back in England probably working on other stories."

"Do you have his phone number?"

"I do." She searched through her phone. "What's your number? I'll send it to you."

Joe recited his number, and she saved it in her phone before forwarding Andrew's number to him. "Your car is one minute away."

Hailey suddenly felt a rush of panic, almost as if she had to tell Joe something before he walked out of her life forever.

He started to turn and stopped. "If…if you remember anything else, you have my number now. Feel free to call me—anytime."

Had he felt it, too, then? Something unsaid between them?

She clasped her phone to her chest. "Yes, yes, I will."

When they reached the front door, he tapped the alarm system on the wall. "Set it."

"I will. Goodbye, Joe."

He raised his hand, and she watched him jog down the first few steps before he made the left turn and disappeared behind the bushes.

She clicked the door closed, locked it and punched in the code to set the alarm system.

She picked up Joe's crushed water bottle and pressed it against her warm face. One brief encounter and she'd constructed a mental picture of Joe McVie as superhero to the rescue.

Snorting, she tossed the bottle into the recycling bin. She'd been fooled by that type before. She rinsed her glass in the sink and sighed at the silence of the house.

The wine had taken the edge off a little, but she still couldn't believe Marten was dead…murdered. Maybe Joe had been wrong about everything.

She walked into the den and turned on the TV, flipping over to the local news. The ten o'clock version hadn't started yet, so she ran upstairs and got ready for bed.

Her face washed, her teeth brushed and her hair in a ponytail, she went back downstairs and tripped on the last step when she caught sight of Marten's hat on the coffee table.

What would've happened if Joe hadn't been around to notice the man tailing her? Would that man have delivered the same warning he'd hoped to convey with the hat? *Keep quiet.*

It was not in her nature to keep quiet. Her father had found that out the hard way.

Helping to ID Marten's body was not endorsing any change of heart he might've had about the statements he'd made regarding their abduction. She hadn't even known Marten was going to retract what he'd claimed about Denver's presence with their captors. Surely, giving a name to an unidentified dead man wouldn't get her in trouble.

She sidled into the den, avoiding the hat, and curled up in a recliner with the remote in her hand. She turned up the sound when the local news started. The incident on the ferry was the top story.

Hailey drew her knees up to her chest and wrapped one arm around her legs. The coast guard hadn't found the body yet, and nobody had reported anyone missing from the ferry. The check of tickets on the boat hadn't completely matched up with the tickets sold. People on the boat must've slipped off without showing their tickets to anyone.

How would they ever identify the man who fell overboard? Would they even believe someone *had* fallen overboard? What evidence did they have?

Even the man's black hat was gone.

Hailey sighed again and turned off the TV. She still had some work to do on a fund-raising gala taking place this week, which would be a good way to get her mind off Marten…and Joe McVie.

She swept her laptop from the kitchen counter and tucked it under her arm as she climbed the stairs. She threw back the covers on her bed and settled cross-legged on the sheet, placing her laptop between her knees.

She tapped her keyboard to get things moving and double clicked the folder that contained her guest list and venue layout. Daisy, her event coordinator, had done most of the work these past few months, booking the hotel ballroom, setting up the catering and the decor. All Hailey had to do was look through everything, approve it and write the checks.

She verified the price for the band Daisy had given her and did another count of the guests. Then she opened her email to send Daisy a message.

Before launching a new email, Hailey skimmed through her messages, deleting most of them. An email with an attachment from something called the Syrian Refugee Campaign caught her eye, and she opened it.

The message had no text except for a link. She almost deleted it, but the subject line jumped out at her. It contained a name—Andrew Reese, the British journalist who'd been captured with her.

She squinted at the date. It had been sent tonight. Maybe it was from Andrew. Maybe he'd heard something about Marten.

Her heart thumped as she clicked the link. A video filled her screen, with no sound or introduction.

The video took her down a long, dark hallway, and Hailey stopped breathing. The blood thrummed in her ears. A door came into focus, and the shaky video continued as someone reached out and opened the door with a gloved hand.

It swung open on a dark room, a single light in the corner, but the camera stayed away from the light, tracking along the shadows instead.

Hailey's fingers curled around the edge of her sheet, bunching the material into her hands. The camera took her farther into the room, suddenly swinging toward an object in the corner under the light.

Hailey gasped at the hooded figure tied to the chair, chin dropped to his or her chest. Was this some kind of sick joke? Some snuff film?

A hand appeared in the frame and whipped the black hood from the person in the chair. The poor soul's head bobbed, but still hung down, long hair obscuring his face.

The hand made its way into the frame again and prodded the man in the chair. Slowly the captive raised his head, looked into the camera from eyes sunken into his swollen face and in a hoarse voice whispered, "Help me, Hailey."

Chapter Four

Joe stretched out on the king-size bed and toed off his shoes. The TV newscast hadn't done much of a story on poor old Marten. Would his body ever wash up?

Joe regretted not getting right to the point with Marten to find out who put Major Denver's name on his lips in the first place. He'd wanted to hold off to see where he went and who he met. He hadn't thought the guy would wind up dead. He'd underestimated the enemy.

A tingle of fear crept across his flesh. Hailey didn't know anything, hadn't retracted her story about hearing one of the terrorists address Denver by name— and now she wouldn't.

His phone, charging next to the bed, rang, and he checked the display. He'd memorized Hailey's number, and he bolted upright to answer her call.

"Hailey, did you remember something?"

"Oh my God, Joe. It's Andrew. They have Andrew now."

"Wait. Slow down. What are you talking about? Who has Andrew?"

"The same people who killed Marten. I'm sure of it. They have Andrew, and they have my email address."

Joe swung his legs off the bed. "Someone sent you an email?"

"It's horrible, Joe. It's Andrew. Th-they've tortured him."

A knot formed in Joe's gut. "This was a video sent to your email address?"

"Yes." Hailey sniffled. "I didn't recognize the email address, but Andrew's name was in the link, so I thought it might be something he was sending. I'm sorry I clicked on it."

"Was anyone else in the video?"

"No, just the cameraman's gloved hand, and I'm pretty sure the video was taken with a phone. It's shaky." She drew in a long breath. "I—I don't know where he is, but we have to help him. We have to call the FBI."

"There are no hints in the video? Background."

"It's horrible, Joe. Andrew's in a room, tied up. They had a hood over his head. When they pulled off the hood, I could tell they'd tortured him, beaten him, but Andrew still mentioned my name."

"He said your name?" Joe launched from the bed and stuffed his feet back into his shoes. He had to see this video for himself.

"He asked me for help." She sobbed. "It was terrible. I'm sick to my stomach."

"I'm coming right over."

"Y-you are? I can forward the video to you."

"I want to see the original email." Did that sound like a good enough excuse? He didn't need an excuse. "You shouldn't be alone right now, Hailey, not after everything that happened tonight."

"If it's not any trouble, I'd appreciate your input."

"Did you set the alarm system on the house?"

"I did."

"Okay. I'm going to download that car app right now and grab a ride over. Fifteen minutes? Don't open the door to anyone else."

"Do you think I'm crazy? I wouldn't open my door to the police chief himself right now."

"Stay in that frame of mind."

Twenty minutes later, Joe bolted from the car and ran up the steps to Hailey's house. He'd texted her from the car, and she must've been watching from the upstairs window. Seconds after he rang the bell, the door swung open.

Hailey grabbed his arm and practically yanked him across the threshold. "Thank you so much. I'm jumping at every little squeak in the house."

He shut the door behind him. "Arm the system."

She reached past him to punch in the code, and he inhaled the fresh scent that matched her fresh face. Devoid of makeup, her hair pulled back, Hailey looked like a college girl—a scared college girl.

"Show me this email and video."

"My laptop's upstairs. I was just going to do a little work on a fund-raiser that my foundation is sponsoring when I tripped across the email." She hugged herself and hunched her shoulders. "I don't know how I'm going to go to sleep with the image of Andrew's poor face in my mind."

She said all of this while climbing the stairs with her head twisted over her shoulder. In her agitation, she tripped a few times, and he put out his hand to steady her so she wouldn't take him with her as she tumbled down the stairs.

He followed her into her bedroom, his gaze riveted by the sway of her hips beneath a very nonsexy pair of flannel pajamas with pink clouds on them.

She turned at the door and pointed to the laptop on the bed as if gesturing toward a rattlesnake ready to strike.

The computer sat at an angle, probably where it landed after she'd pushed it from her lap.

He sat on the edge of the bed and pulled the laptop toward him. "Is the video up?"

"It should be. I didn't close it out or turn it off." She crept up and hovered over his shoulder, one bare foot on top of the other.

Joe tapped the keyboard, and the still of a dark hallway appeared on the monitor. He clicked the arrow in the lower-left corner and watched the sickening display with a dry mouth.

Hailey had backed up and turned away before the video ended and stood across the room twisting her fingers in front of her. "What do you think?"

"These are some seriously sick people." He didn't tell Hailey he'd seen a lot worse. Of course, she'd been at that refugee center when it had been bombed. She'd seen a lot worse, too.

"Can we report this to someone?"

"The police aren't going to know what to do with it, but you can call the FBI. Do you still have the contact info of the agents who interviewed you when you got back?"

"I have their cards. I'll call them tomorrow. Do you think they can do anything?"

"They can at least touch base with their British counterparts if Andrew is in England and this occurred there. They may be able to do some computer forensics and find out where this came from."

"And why?" She crossed her arms over her midsection. "I have to know why this is happening. Why Marten? Why Andrew? Why me?"

"You all have one thing in common."

"We were all kidnapped by the terrorist group that bombed the refugee camp and destroyed the peace talks."

"And in one way or another, you all called out Major Denver as being one of them." Joe closed the video and shut the lid of the laptop, as if that could keep the horror away from Hailey. "What about the other two? Have you had any contact with Naraj and Ayala since the incident?"

"Not with Naraj. I exchanged a few emails with Ayala just to check on things at the center, send some money and tell her about the fund-raiser."

"When was the last time you heard from her?"

Hailey's dark eyes got huge in her face. "A few weeks ago."

"Did she mention anything out of the ordinary?"

"No. Should I contact her again?"

"You don't have to tell her what's going on over here. Just feel her out."

"I'll do that now." She waved a hand at the laptop. "Is the video off?"

"I closed it and the email." He opened the computer and turned around to face her. "It won't bite."

She approached the bed and dropped to her knees. Using the bed as a table, she launched her email and typed a message to Ayala. "I'm just asking her for a progress report and an accounting of the money I sent. I need that for my tax guy, anyway."

She hit the send button with a flourish. "I'd better not find out anything has happened to Ayala, or I'm going to lose it. Do you think Andrew's okay? Did those injuries look life-threatening to you? They're not going to kill him, are they?"

"Like they killed Marten?"

Covering her mouth, she sat back on her heels. "What do they want, Joe? Do they want to shut us up? We're not saying anything—at least, Andrew and I aren't saying anything."

"You don't know what Andrew has or hasn't said."

"Are you trying to tell me he also retracted his story about Denver? Someone is going to a lot of trouble to keep driving that narrative forward."

"You have no idea." Joe bent his head forward and pinched the tight muscle at the back of his neck.

Hailey braced her hands on her thighs. "It's more than us, isn't it? They have more on Denver than just a few aid workers implicating him in a bombing, don't they?"

"There's a whole framework around him." He shifted to the side and patted the bed. "Come up off the floor and have a seat."

Her gaze darted to the spot he'd indicated, and she licked her lips.

Was she afraid of him? Afraid he'd make a move. She had called him when she got the video, so she must trust him on some level—maybe just not the sitting-with-him-on-her-bed level.

He pushed off the bed and grabbed the laptop. "Where do you want this?"

"You can plug it into the charger on the nightstand." Rising, she wrapped her ponytail around her hand but still didn't sit on the bed. "I'm going to call the FBI tomorrow morning. Do you want to be there when they question me? If they question me?"

"I'm sure they will want to talk to you, but I'm not gonna be there. I don't want any government official to know I'm involved in this. I'm supposedly on leave, and I don't think my superiors would appreciate my interference."

"You're not the only one…interfering, are you? You said they have more evidence against Denver that others debunked?"

"They do, and two of my Delta Force team members were able to poke holes in that evidence, but that hasn't cleared Denver's name or changed the course of this investigation. We need names. We need motives. Right now I have no idea why anyone would want to set up Denver."

"I wish I could help you. How *can* I help you?"

Joe raised his brows at Hailey, arms folded, clutching the material of her pink-cloud pajamas. "Why do you want to help? Why do you go to places like Syria? It's dangerous. You could be playing tennis and lunching like most rich women do."

She tilted her head to the side, and her ponytail swung over her shoulder. "Is that your image of most rich women?"

"That's what they seemed to be doing in Beacon Hill all the time."

"And you know this how?"

He shrugged. "My mom used to clean house for them."

Hailey blinked. "Oh. Well, some of us do more than that. I don't even like tennis."

"You must have something driving you. Guilt?"

A pink tint crept from her neck to her face, matching her pajamas. "What does that mean?"

"I don't know. Some rich people feel guilty about being rich and then try to make up for it by doing philanthropic stuff." He jerked his thumb at her laptop on the bedside table. "Like fund-raisers and running off to dangerous countries to try to make a difference."

Hailey bit her bottom lip, her face still flushed.

"I'm sorry. That was rude." He took a turn around the bedroom. "I don't care what your motives are and they're none of my business anyway. You're obviously generous with your money *and* your time and willing to take risks to make a difference. That's more than most people do. I respect that."

"I didn't take offense." She flicked her ponytail back over her shoulder. "Crazy rich people and their money. But I really was serious about wanting to help. Why wouldn't I? Marten has been murdered. Andrew is in danger. What next?"

Joe clenched his jaw. He didn't want to scare her any more than she already was, but *she* just might be next. "Maybe the FBI can tell you when you talk to them tomorrow. I guess I should be going."

He didn't want to leave her, but he couldn't exactly invite himself to spend the night. She'd be safe here with her tricked-out alarm system and cameras.

"Should I—should I tell you what happens after I talk to them?"

"If you don't mind. I'm going to try to look into Andrew Reese on my own—at least find out what he told the army about Denver and if he had a change of heart lately."

Joe started backing out of the room, waiting for one sign from Hailey that she wanted him to stay.

"I'll call you tomorrow. Thanks so much for showing up tonight. That video creeped me out."

"It would creep anyone out. Do you feel okay now? Safe?"

"I do. I'm fine."

They said goodbye for the second time that night, and Joe assured Hailey that he'd call for a car when he got to the bottom of her steps.

Instead, once he hit the sidewalk, he rubbed his hands together and huddled into his jacket. He loped across the street and stationed himself on a bench bordering a small park with a view of the bay…and Hailey's house.

Hell, morning wasn't far off anyway, and if he couldn't be guarding Hailey from inside the place, he'd guard her from outside. Either way, she *did* need guarding. And he'd just appointed himself the man for the job.

THE NEXT MORNING Hailey woke with a start. She sat up, her heart pounding in her chest. Marten. Andrew.

She threw off the bedcovers and padded to the window. As she peeked through a crack in the drapes, she saw a man with reddish hair ducking into the back seat of a car.

She curled her fingers around the material of the drapes as the car sped off. Then she blinked. That was Joe in the car. Had he tried coming over this morning?

She spun around and grabbed her laptop, plopping back down on the messy covers of the bed. She'd better get used to accessing her security footage, anyway.

She brought up the video of her front porch and

scanned back through the previous half hour—nothing, nobody. If Joe hadn't been at her front door, what had he been doing on her block?

She fell back on her bed, the computer still resting on her thighs. What did Joe hope to accomplish? If someone embedded in the army or the government, as Joe had implied, wanted to paint Major Rex Denver as a traitor, the words of some lowly aid worker were not going to stop that train.

Huffing out a breath, she draped an arm over her forehead. Joe burned to do the right thing. She could understand that sentiment. She had the same fire.

She showered and dressed and then turned on the TV news when she got downstairs. Marten's body still hadn't been found in the bay, and authorities were beginning to question whether anyone actually went overboard or if a few passengers had overactive imaginations.

But she had Marten's hat. Her gaze darted to his familiar headgear still perched on top of the coffee table. She planned to tell the FBI everything today.

After breakfast, she placed a call to one of the agents who'd interviewed her when she returned from Syria and left a message. Avoiding the email with the video of Andrew, she returned to the work she'd planned to get done on the fund-raiser last night. When her phone rang, she jumped.

She'd programmed Joe's name and number into her phone, and seeing that name now sent a warm ribbon of relief down her spine. "Hi, Joe."

"Everything okay this morning?"

"As right as it can be with Marten presumed dead and Andrew bruised and battered probably somewhere in England."

"No more emails or late-night visits to your porch?"

She swirled her coffee in the mug. "Nobody but you."

Joe sucked in an audible breath.

"That was you this morning getting into a car, wasn't it?"

"Guilty."

"You spent the night outside my house?"

"Technically across the street from your house."

"Are you nuts? If you thought it was a good idea to keep watch over me last night, why didn't you say so? You could've spent the night on the couch or in one of the many bedrooms in this house."

"Hailey, we'd just met. I didn't want to crowd you."

"You also didn't want to worry me. You really believe I need a bodyguard?"

"A lot happened yesterday. We didn't know if they were finished warning you or not. Just playing it safe."

"Well, thanks, but now I feel guilty."

"Do you always automatically feel guilty about everything?"

Hailey clasped her hand around her cup. Joe obviously never had any reason to feel guilty about anything.

"Okay, scratch that. Not guilty, but you should've told me. You must've been freezing out there, and I could've at least offered you breakfast." Maybe she would've offered him much more than that.

"I've stood watch under worse conditions, and I had breakfast at my hotel. Did you call the FBI yet?"

Hailey let out a silent breath. Joe McVie was all business. Even if she had offered more, he probably would've turned her down. "I left a message with one of the agents. He hasn't called back yet."

"I did a little research this morning on Andrew Reese."

"Already? Did you get any sleep?"

"A little." Joe coughed and continued as if to brush off his lack of shut-eye. "The only thing I could find on Andrew was a story he wrote about Syria for an online geography journal. He did report on the bombing of the refugee camp and the effect it had on the peace progress."

"Maybe that was enough to get him noticed. I'm not doing anything to get noticed."

"Are you sure? What's this fund-raiser you mentioned?"

Hailey swallowed. "I-it's for the children of Syria affected by the civil war."

Joe's silence hung over the line between them.

"Who could object to that?" As soon as she uttered the words, she answered her own question. "The very people who indiscriminately bombed those refugees."

"Can you cancel it?"

"Cancel it? It's scheduled for this week. There's no

way I can cancel. Too much work has already gone into the event—invitations sent, money spent."

"Watch your back."

"Thanks for stating the obvious." Hailey cleared her throat. "Would you like to come and watch my back for me?"

"At the fund-raiser?"

"It's just a party for rich people—food, music, dancing. I have to give them something for their generous donations. Your donation can be my safety."

"You want me to be your bodyguard?"

"How about my date?" She held her breath.

"A bodyguard posing as your date."

All business. "Sure, if you want to think of it that way—but the date part requires a tux."

Joe snorted. "Damn, forgot to pack one of mine."

"I can send you to my dad's tailor to get suited up. He'll do it quickly and put it on my dad's account."

"I don't—"

She cut him off. "Listen, McVie. I'm not going to pay you for this bodyguarding gig, so you might as well take what you can get—and that's a tux."

"Yes, ma'am. Where is this tailor?"

"Mission District. I'll give you the address and let Tony know as soon as we get off the phone. He'll hook you up."

"You're your father's daughter after all."

"If I were my father's daughter, you'd be paying for the tux and thanking me for it."

As soon as she ended the call with Joe, she placed

one to Tony, her father's longtime tailor, and gave him the heads-up on Joe. Then she returned to her laptop, flexing her fingers before launching her email. She didn't need any more surprises this morning.

Sucking in her bottom lip, she scrolled through the new messages. When she reached the end, she slumped against the sofa cushion. No more torture videos.

She picked out the message from last night and wrinkled her nose. The little paper clip indicating an attachment had disappeared from the email icon.

With a sweaty palm, she grasped the mouse and double clicked on the message—nothing in the body and no attachment.

Had she deleted it by accident? Her pulse racing, she searched her deleted items and then all the videos on her laptop. Not that she wanted to see Andrew's battered face again, but she needed some evidence to show the FBI.

She pushed the computer from her lap and jumped up from the couch. How had they done that? How had they gotten into her computer and removed a file?

She jerked as her phone rang, and then she lunged for it. When she saw the FBI's number on the display, she blew out a breath.

"Ms. Duvall? This is Agent Porter returning your call."

Hailey's gaze shifted to the laptop abandoned on the couch. "I need to meet with you—today."

"Is this regarding the incident at the refugee camp?"

Hailey squeezed her eyes closed for a second. "I think so. Did you hear about the man who fell off the Alcatraz ferry last night?"

Porter paused for two heartbeats. "Let's not discuss this on the phone. We'll meet you this afternoon."

"Now. We need to meet now."

"Name a place close to the Financial District and we'll be there."

"Do you know Caffé Luce on Columbus?"

"We'll be there in thirty minutes."

Hailey placed a call to Joe and put her phone on speaker as she scrambled around the room, stuffing her laptop in its case and her feet into a pair of boots.

Joe answered after several rings. "Are you checking up on me? I'll be heading out to Tony the tailor's in a few hours."

"It's not that. The video from last night showing Andrew is gone. Someone deleted it from my computer remotely—at least I hope it was remotely—and I'm on my way to a meeting with the FBI."

Joe whistled. "At their offices downtown?"

"No, we're meeting at Caffé Luce in Little Italy."

"You won't have anything to show them."

"No, but I'll have plenty to tell them."

"I don't have to ask you not to say anything about me, do I?"

"Don't worry, but I am going to tell them about

Marten last night and the video. I mean, they have to be connected, right? Why would anyone care about what happened in Syria? It happened. The terrorists were successful. Why revisit it now?"

"Because there are elements about that incident that someone doesn't want revealed."

"I know. I know. Major Denver's involvement—or rather, noninvolvement."

"Get to your meeting. I'll get fitted for my tux."

"I'm going to tell them everything—except about your presence here."

"You should. Keep me posted."

"Lunch later?"

"Yeah, a debriefing."

Debriefing? Joe was determined to keep their... relationship on neutral territory. "Yeah, whatever. And, Joe?"

"Yes?"

"No velvet on the tux."

She ended the call and strapped a purse across her body. She didn't have enough time to catch public transportation, and she had no intention of driving and trying to find a place to park, so she called up a car on her phone.

Fifteen minutes later, she stepped out of the car and jogged across the street to Caffé Luce. One look around the half-empty coffeehouse, crowded with small tables, told her she was a little early.

She ordered a cappuccino and cupped the big mug

in her hands as she carried it to a table outside. She set it down and dragged a wrought-iron chair from another table to hers. Agent Porter had mentioned that *they* were going to meet her. FBI agents usually traveled in pairs, so he must be bringing his sidekick, Agent Winston.

Two suits with matching Ray-Bans hustled up the sidewalk, and Hailey lifted her hand to Agent Porter. She'd discovered the man had played football at Stanford, and he still carried himself like an athlete.

The two agents stopped at her table, and Porter said, "We'll go inside to get some coffee. Do you want a refill?"

She tapped her cup. "All set."

Hailey watched the thin crowd on the sidewalk— too late for morning rush hour and too early for lunch…also known as debriefing, according to Joe McVie.

Her head jerked up at the squeal from a car's tires, and her eyes narrowed behind her sunglasses as she watched some idiot making a U-turn where six streets intersected. The car continued to careen down the street and swerved sharply.

Hailey's heart slammed against her chest as the car leaped the curb, one set of its wheels on the sidewalk.

The out-of-control driver plowed through some foliage and knocked over a wooden sign, and still he kept coming straight toward the tables on the sidewalk... straight for her.

Chapter Five

Joe's legs were pumping before the car even hit the sidewalk. By the time he made it to the other side of the street, several tables had been knocked on their sides, their spindly legs pointing at the sky.

Hailey, wide-eyed and white-faced, had plastered herself against the side of the building, debris from the wreckage at her feet.

The blue sedan that had jumped the curb squealed in Reverse, and Joe threw himself at the hood. The driver punched the accelerator. The car disappeared from beneath him, and Joe landed on the sidewalk in a belly flop, the smell of burning rubber and exhaust scorching his lungs.

"Joe!" A hand grabbed the back of his shirt and practically ripped it off him.

He rolled to his side and squinted up at Hailey looming over him, her sunglasses shoved to the top of her head.

"Are you crazy? He could've run you over."

"Did you get a license number?" He scrambled to

his feet, smacking his hands together to dislodge the grit embedded in his palms.

"It's running through my head right now." Hailey held up one incredibly steady finger. "Wait."

As she dashed inside the coffeehouse, sirens wailed down the street, and the two FBI agents Hailey was meeting hovered over the scene.

They wouldn't recognize him, would they? He'd never met them before, but he could bet they'd know his name and his connection with Major Denver. Joe ducked his head.

Hailey rushed back to the sidewalk, waving a white napkin with not a hint of surrender on her face. "I have it. I have the license plate."

The two agents approached her, and the tall African American spoke first. "Are you all right? Did a car come up on the sidewalk? From inside it sounded like an explosion."

Hailey's gaze darted from the agent in front of her to Joe. He shook his head once.

"Yeah, the car jumped the curb, and I know why."

The agent's eyes bugged out from their sockets. "You think it was deliberate?"

In a harsh whisper just loud enough for Joe to hear several feet away, she said, "Someone was trying to stop our meeting, trying to stop me."

The agent lifted his shoulders. "Ms. Duvall, nobody knows about this meeting."

"I wouldn't count on that." She flicked the napkin

in his face. "I got the car's license number, and I'm giving it to the police."

The agents hadn't noticed him, so Joe busied himself with brushing off his jeans and then helping the store's employees right the tables and chairs.

A cop car pulled up to the curb, and an officer stepped out. Before the cop could get one word out of his mouth, Hailey rushed up to him with her napkin.

"I got the license plate."

"Slow down." He plucked the napkin from her fingers. "What happened here?"

Hailey launched into her description of the events and jabbed her finger at the napkin in the officer's hand when she reached the end of her narrative. "That's the license number of the car, a blue four-door sedan."

"Nobody was hurt?"

"I was the only one sitting outside, and the car didn't reach the building."

"Did the driver lose control of the car? Did he ever get out of the vehicle?"

"It was a hit-and-run. He rammed the tables, backed up and took off." Hailey licked her lips and flicked a gaze at Joe. "It might have been deliberate. I was here to meet with a couple of FBI agents about… another matter."

The officer raised his brows as the agents crowded Joe and Hailey.

"Ms. Duvall, we'd like to talk to the officer privately for a few moments. We'd still like to hear what you have to say. Can you meet us inside? All this—" the agent swept his arm across the scene "—hasn't scared you off, has it?"

"Absolutely not." She charged past the agents and into the coffeehouse.

Joe followed, hot on her heels, and leaned over her shoulder at the counter as she ordered another cappuccino. "Add a black coffee to go to that order and I'll pay for both."

Hailey cranked her head around. "Are you okay after that stunt you pulled?"

"Stunt? I was trying to stop the car. I figured I could drag the guy out and get some answers from him."

"Looked like he was ready to drag you down the street under his wheels. We'll leave it up to the police to get answers."

"Do you really think that car is going to come back to the person who tried to interrupt your meeting with the FBI?"

Her cheeks flushed, and she flicked her bangs from her eyes. "So you believe me?"

"Oh, yeah. That was a warning. Would he have done that with the FBI agents sitting next to you? I'm not sure about that, but he saw an opportunity and took it."

"Someone must be following me." Her gaze tracked over his shoulder and scanned the street behind him. "Do they really think that's going to scare me off?"

"I'm sure it would do the trick for anyone else." Hearing the agents' voices, Joe put his finger to his lips as he reached past her and grabbed his coffee. "Remember, keep my name out of this."

She shot a glance at the two Fibbies coming through the door. "Got it."

Raising the cup to his lips, he whispered through the steam, "Meet me at the tailor's shop when you're done."

She nodded and then lifted her chin toward the two agents. "Table by the window?"

Joe slipped out of the coffeehouse and sipped from his cup as he leaned against the pole listing the schedule at the bus stop.

Hailey would have quite a story to tell those agents, but would they believe her with no proof? And could they protect her, or would that be up to him?

AN HOUR LATER Hailey yanked open the door of the tailor her father had used for almost thirty years and tripped to a stop. A dapper man in a black tux tugged on the cuffs of his shirt and did a half turn in front of the mirror.

"Are you sure this slim fit is the thing?"

"It's made for a build like yours, sir."

Hailey dabbed the corner of her mouth to make sure no drool had escaped and then strode across the floor of the small shop.

"Working your magic, Tony?"

"He's got the physique this particular designer had in mind when he created this tux."

Joe shrugged out of the jacket. "Tony doesn't have anything cheap in here, but you probably know that."

"Don't worry about it. I told you this is your payment. After you sit through that boring evening, you're going to understand that I'm coming out ahead in this deal."

"How'd the meeting go?"

"I'll tell you over lunch." She ran a hand across a rack of jackets, the silky material sliding through her fingers. "Are you almost done with him, Tony?"

"I will return him to you as soon as he picks out a vest, and then he's all yours."

Hailey's mouth watered at the prospect of Joe McVie being all hers.

Joe unbuttoned his pants, and her mouth watered even more.

"I'm done. Maybe Hailey will do the honors and pick out something for me while I get dressed. I trust her taste a lot more than mine." He retreated behind the dressing room curtain.

"He's lying, you know." Tony winked as he gathered his tape measure and pins.

"About?" Wouldn't be the first time or the last a man lied to her.

"Joe has impeccable taste."

"Then I'd better do him justice." Hailey selected a black vest for Joe. He didn't need any colors or gimmicks to show off. The man could shine wearing nothing but his skivvies—and she might even pay to see that.

She signed off on the purchase just as Joe made

his way out of the dressing room, the slacks and shirt draped over one arm.

He dropped them on the counter, and Hailey shoved them toward Tony. "Joe told you this was a rush job, didn't he?"

"He did. Good thing he mentioned your name before he said he wanted it in a hurry or I would've told him to hit the bricks."

She squeezed Tony's arm. "Now you're the liar. You'd never tell a customer to get lost, but I appreciate your service, Tony."

As she and Joe stepped through the door, Tony called after her, "Give my best to your father."

"Will do." She waved behind her.

Joe took her arm. "Back to business."

"And lunch. Chinese? We can walk to Chinatown from here."

"I could use some fresh air."

Hailey kept the conversation casual as they strolled to Chinatown, and Joe didn't seem to mind the chit-chat after all his talk about business. Why was he so afraid to mix a little pleasure with their work?

They joined the hustle and bustle of Chinatown, the sights, smells and sounds putting an end to any communication between them except for the occasional jab in the ribs or a pointing finger.

When Hailey spotted Superior Best, her favorite Chinese restaurant, she tugged on Joe's sleeve and leaned in close. "We're eating there."

They cut sideways through the crowd and ducked into the dark embrace of the restaurant.

Lottie Chu, matriarch of the Chu family and its businesses, greeted Hailey with a spark in her dark eyes and a curt nod. "Table for two, Hailey?"

"Yes, please, Lottie. This is my...friend Joe."

Lottie clasped the ornate menus to her chest, drumming her fingernails on the embossed covers and narrowing her eyes. "You a good friend to Hailey, Joe?"

"I think I've been a good friend so far, but you'll have to ask Hailey."

Hailey rolled her eyes. "Joe's a good guy, Lottie. Can we please sit down now?"

The old woman hunched her thin shoulders and led them to a table in the back of the room. She smacked the menus on the table. "Sit. Good table for good guy."

When Lottie turned and scurried to the front door to intercept a family of tourists, Joe pulled out Hailey's chair and swiped the back of his hand across his brow. "Whew. I'm glad I sort of passed that test."

"I've known Lottie for years." Hailey turned over her teacup and whipped the napkin into her lap. "My father used to take me here when I was a little girl, and Lottie has gotten somewhat protective over the years."

"Yeah, just a little. She seemed ready to bite my head off, though she doesn't even look five feet tall."

"She's not, but don't let her size fool you." Hailey thanked the waiter for the tea and held the pot over Joe's cup. "Tea?"

"Sure."

She shoved one of the heavy menus toward him. "Any preferences?"

"I'll let you do the honors—just no octopus or anything else I can't identify on my plate."

"I'll stick to chicken, beef and pork."

When the waiter returned, Hailey ordered some safe dishes and then picked up her teacup and inhaled the light scent of the green tea before taking a sip. "The car was stolen."

"Figures." Joe slammed the cup back into the saucer, and his tea sloshed into the saucer.

"That license plate I was so proud of identifying? It came back to a stolen car from San Jose. One of the officers told us that while we were still at the coffeehouse."

"That doesn't surprise me." Joe dragged the napkin from his lap and wiped the tea from his hand. "Were there any cameras? Did the coffeehouse or any of the other businesses have cameras on the street?"

"They did, and the police may or may not look at that footage."

"You're telling me they're not taking this very seriously."

"That's right—a single-car accident, he didn't injure anyone and the damage was minimal, even though it was a hit-and-run." She clinked her cup back into the saucer. "I thought they might at least want to recover the stolen car, but I guess it's not a high priority right now. I also suggested that the guy might be a terrorist just to light a fire under them, but since the sidewalk was mostly empty—except for me—the police didn't buy that theory."

"And the FBI? Did the agents believe it might be someone trying to stop your meeting with them?"

She wrinkled her nose. "They didn't discount that idea, but I guess they would've been more convinced if I'd wound up dead."

"Too bad you had to disappoint them." He drained the small teacup, which looked like a thimble in his hand. "You told them about Marten and Andrew?"

"I did, but there's still no proof Marten was ever on that ferry, and they're not interested in his black hat. There's not even any proof that someone went overboard."

"And you don't have that video with Andrew to show them."

She smacked the edge of the table with her fingertips. "I should've sent it to them as soon as I received it. I should've sent it to you."

"You had no idea someone would wipe it clean from your computer, but I should've thought of that and had you send it to me."

"I had no idea that was even a thing." She smiled at the waiter as he rolled a cart up to their table with a host of covered dishes.

Joe's eyes widened. "Is there an army you plan to feed when we're done?"

"I thought you might be hungry after all the excitement today." She rubbed her hands together as the Szechuan spices tickled her nose. "I know I am."

"I took you for one of those women who eat a stalk of celery and one cracker and call it a day."

"Ah, the narcissistic socialite type you ran into on Beacon Hill." She dug into the kung pao chicken and ladled it over her steamed rice. "Should I be offended?"

"I know damn well you're not a narcissistic socialite. No socialite I know would put herself in danger to help others halfway around the world."

"Know many socialites other than the ones your mom worked for?"

"Um, not really." He sucked some sauce off the edge of his thumb. "But now you're the gold standard of all socialites."

Heat rose to her cheeks and she hadn't even sampled the spicy entrées yet. "Anyway, I'm tall and naturally skinny, and I do like running up and down these hills in the city."

Joe cleared his throat and dipped his chin to his chest, as if he'd just become aware that their banter had veered toward the personal and she'd given him too much information.

"So, the agents didn't believe you." Joe scrutinized his forkful of food before putting it in his mouth.

"I wouldn't say that, but without any proof that someone is offing the aid workers who were duped into bombing the refugee camp, there's not much they can do. You know how it goes."

"Nobody brought up my name, did they?"

"You don't trust me?" She pinched a piece of chicken between her chopsticks.

"I trust you. I'm just curious as to whether or not I'm on their radar. I told you that two of my Delta Force team members have already delved into the mystery behind Major Denver's actions. I'm wondering if the FBI or CIA has started connecting the dots yet."

"There are dots to connect? Is this a planned and concerted investigation?"

"Planned and concerted?" Joe shook his head. "Try haphazard and blundering, but we're all committed to doing our part to look into what we know is a setup. Denver would do no less for one of us."

"Nobody mentioned your name or Denver's. I told them I thought someone was trying to keep the four of us quiet, starting with Marten and continuing with Andrew and even taking a chance on me right before the meeting."

"Speaking of the four of you, have you heard back from the nurse yet?"

"Not yet." Hailey checked her phone just to make sure Ayala hadn't sent her an email in the past hour.

"Did you offer any suggestions for the motive behind these attacks?"

"I did not, and the agents wondered the same. While they didn't dismiss my fears out of hand, they did question why someone would want to muzzle us."

"After what my two teammates discovered about Denver so far, I would've thought they might put two and two together. But that would require them to think outside the box and to entertain the idea that some-one on the inside—CIA, DoD, the army or maybe even their own agency—has some kind of vendetta against Denver."

"I can tell you right now, that's not how they're thinking." She aimed a chopstick at his plate. "Do you like the food?"

"It's great—better with this." He held up his fork. "Gets the food to my stomach faster than chopsticks."

"I knew you'd be hungry." She placed her chopsticks across the edge of her plate. "So, the FBI is no use, al-though the agents did say they'd look into Andrew's whereabouts."

"And Marten's? They could start with his phone. Did you tell them someone texted you from Marten's phone after the ferry incident?"

"They're going to put in an order to ping his phone."

"Have you tried texting the phone since the time right after the incident on the ferry?"

"I've texted him a few times, but there's been no response, and they don't look like they're being de-livered."

"More tea, Hailey?" Lottie had returned to the table with the check on a tray with some fortune cookies. She placed the tray firmly in front of Joe.

Hailey covered her smile with her hand. "None for me. Lunch was delicious as usual. You could send the waiter back here with some to-go boxes, though."

Lottie raised her hand over her head and snapped her fingers. "Danny. Boxes over here."

Joe made a show of grabbing the check and taking out his wallet.

Lottie looked down her nose and pursed her lips into a smile. "Good guy. You keep, Hailey."

Laughing, Hailey shook her head at Joe, whose face almost matched the red wallpaper in the restaurant, which was a couple of shades brighter than his hair. "He's not mine to keep, Lottie."

"Maybe you see it in fortune." Lottie tapped the tray, and the fortune cookies jumped.

When Lottie scurried away to another table, Joe held up a twenty-dollar bill. "Do you think this is a big enough tip? Lottie scares me."

"She's just toying with us. She likes to play the role of tiger mom for the tourists, but she's actually an extremely astute and modern businesswoman. Her son and daughter run the family's financial empire now, but Lottie is the one who grew it."

"I can believe that."

Danny, clearly in awe of Lottie himself, not only brought over the to-go containers, but he filled them up with their leftovers. Once he'd bagged them, Joe handed him the check along with several bills.

Hailey wiggled her fingers over the cookies. "I love fortune cookies. Superior Best gets theirs from the fortune cookie factory around the corner, so they're super fresh."

Joe snatched one of the cookies from beneath her fingers and cracked it open. "Ah, but are they accurate?"

"Well?" She tapped a chopstick against Joe's tea-cup. "What does yours say?"

His eyes widened, and he twisted his head around to track Lottie's flitting progress across the restaurant. "She planted this."

"Not possible. C'mon, out with it."

Pinching the little slip of paper between his thumb and forefinger, he read aloud. "'You will meet a dark-haired beauty. Take a chance.'"

"No! You're lying." She snatched the fortune from his fingers and held it up to her face. The exact words he'd just read danced before her eyes. "I wouldn't put it past Lottie, but I don't see how she could've managed that. I could've picked that one."

"Could've gone either way." Joe batted his eyelashes at her. "Are you implying I'm no dark-haired beauty?"

"It didn't say dark *red*." She crumpled up the piece of paper and threw it at him.

He caught it and closed his fist around it. "Let's see what yours is, and then we'll know for sure if Lottie tampered with the fortunes."

With a smile playing about her lips, Hailey broke the remaining cookie in two and pulled the slip of paper from one half. As she read the words, her mouth twisted, killing her smile.

"What's wrong?"

"It's just one of those stupid, generic fortunes that could apply to anyone." She dropped the fortune as if it scorched her fingertips.

"No tall red-haired strangers in your future?" Joe swept up the piece of paper, a frown creasing his brow.

He read this one aloud, too, but he didn't have to. Hailey had already memorized it.

"'Be on the lookout for coming events. They cast their shadows beforehand.'" He dropped the fortune, and it floated to the table. "You're right—just silliness. I guess Lottie didn't rig the cookies."

"Coming events casting shadows? That sounds ominous." She flicked the piece of paper away from her— the farther, the better.

"Hailey." He entwined his fingers with hers. "Those are printed words someone baked into a cookie around the corner."

"Yeah, I know that." She bit into the cookie, catching a shower of crumbs with her hand. "I just don't think I've ever gotten a serious fortune like that one before."

"I get those all the time." He smoothed out his own fortune with his thumb. "It's the sexy ones like this I never get."

She cracked a smile, feeling like an idiot. She may have a lot of problems right now, but a warning from a cookie wasn't one of them.

Her phone buzzed, and as she reached for it, she noticed Joe folding his fortune and slipping it into his wallet. He'd probably done that to make her feel better.

Uneasiness fluttered in her belly as she glanced at her phone's display. "I don't know what this number is, but it's local. Hello?"

A man's voice answered, his words carrying a slight accent. "Is this Hailey Duvall?"

"Yes, it is. Who's this?" She shrugged her shoulders at Joe's raised eyebrows.

"My name is Joost Palstra. I'm a friend of Marten's."

Hailey gripped the phone tighter. "Have you seen Marten lately? We were supposed to get together and he never showed."

Joe tapped the leg of her chair with his foot and she held up her finger.

"I saw Marten yesterday afternoon. He was staying with me. That's why I'm calling. He took off, but he left some stuff here."

"D-did he tell you he was going somewhere?"

"You know Marten, sketchy on the details. Anyway, he did ask me to call you if he didn't return, so I'm doing that, but I'm thinking his disappearance might be related to his gambling."

Hailey's heart stuttered. "What makes you think that?"

"He has a lot of people looking for him all of a sudden—and they don't look like the type of guys you want to disappoint."

Chapter Six

Hailey's eyes grew round, and she put one hand over her heart.

Joe shoved a napkin and pen toward her and tapped on the napkin with his fingertip.

As she continued to talk to Marten's friend, she scribbled on the napkin.

Joe squinted at the words she'd written—*people looking for Marten*—and cocked his head. If they'd killed him, why would they be looking for him?

Before he could write a question back, Hailey ended the conversation on the phone.

Snatching the napkin back, she said, "Marten had been staying with Joost and told him to call me if he didn't return, but now people are looking for Marten."

"Wait." Joe held up his hands. "Is this guy at a hotel?"

"A hotel? No." Hailey looked up, pen poised above the napkin. "Why do you think that?"

"Don't forget, I followed Marten from the airport. He went to a hotel in some ritzy area of the city—Nob

Hill, I think. That's how I tracked him to the Alcatraz ferry last night. He wasn't staying with anyone." He leveled a finger at her phone. "How do you know this guy is legit and not trying to lure you into a trap?"

"Marten has mentioned this friend before, and why would he warn me about unsavory characters searching for Marten if he *were* an unsavory character?"

"Maybe to gain your trust. Does this Joost know who these people are?"

She wrote an address on the back of the napkin. "Nope, just that they're pretty shady looking."

"Joost..." He stopped and scratched his chin. "What kinda name is Joost, anyway?"

"He's Dutch, like Marten. Has a very slight accent."

"So... Joost didn't think there was anything strange about Marten not returning to his place?"

"Marten warned him that he might be taking off at any time and told him if he did, he was supposed to call me."

"And tell you what?"

"That he wants me to pick up whatever Marten left behind." Hailey's gaze had locked onto her crumpled fortune on the table. "Joost wants me to come by and get Marten's stuff."

"From your side of the conversation, I gather you're going to pick it up now at Joost's place?"

"Of course. Whatever Marten left for me might contain a clue or something as to what he was doing here and why he wanted to see me."

"You're not going alone." He jerked his thumb over

his shoulder at the plate-glass windows overlooking the chaos of Chinatown. "There still might be someone following you, although I kept a close watch on the way over here."

She put a hand over her mouth. "You were watching to see if we had a tail? I didn't even notice. Why didn't you let me in on it?"

"And make it obvious that I was on the lookout? We weren't followed here, and we're not going to be followed to Joost's." He gulped down some water and put the glass on top of the fortune that had spooked Hailey. "Where does he live and how do we get there?"

"He's in the Sunset District. We'll need a car to get there." Hailey picked up the bag containing their leftover food and swung it from her fingers. "I suppose I can't lug this around the city."

"We can have the car make a stop at your place and put it in the fridge. Then we can pick up your car at the same time."

"That's okay. I don't want to drive over, and I know how to make good use of the food without throwing it away." She pointed to the cell phone in his hand. "You want to order a car on that app? Have him pick us up two blocks down so he doesn't have to drive into this mess."

"Sure." While he tapped his phone, Hailey spoke with Lottie and put something in the bag with the food.

On the way out the door, Joe waved to Lottie, who

gave him a secret smile. She *had* planted that fortune, and he just might follow its advice.

They meandered down the sidewalk, their pace slowed by the tourists ducking in and out of the shops and restaurants that lined the streets.

When they reached the end of Chinatown, Hailey tapped his arm. "Hang on. I'll be right back."

He watched her walk, her long stride eating up the pavement beneath her feet, the plastic bag banging against her leg. When she reached a small park, she cut in toward a set of benches where a couple of homeless guys were lounging. She held out the bag to the man on the first bench, said a few words and spun around, heading back toward him.

Joe mumbled under his breath, "Do-gooder."

Hailey reached him seconds before their car pulled up to the curb. He got the door for her, and as she slid onto the back seat, he asked, "Do you do that often?"

"Give my leftovers to the homeless? When it's convenient for me to do so, like today."

"Yeah, right. Don't downplay your charitable heart." He squeezed her knee. "I told you, I'm impressed as hell."

The driver twisted his head over his shoulder. "How are you folks doing today? Sunset?"

"Yes." Hailey pulled the napkin from her pocket and rattled off Joost's address. Then she turned to Joe. "I hope he's there before we are. He was on his way home."

"We'll wait for him outside. At least it's not raining."

The driver sped up and down the hilly streets until they reached wider roads with more suburban-type housing.

Joe pressed his hand against the window. "This is different."

"This area's a little more residential. Joost lives in the garage apartment of a house. He told me to go around the side of the house for his front door. There are a lot of rentals like that here—cheaper."

The driver pulled up to a light blue clapboard house with a motorcycle parked on one side of the driveway.

They exited the car and circled around to the side of the house.

"That's it." Hailey gestured toward a sliding glass door. "That's his front door."

"What do we do? Knock on the glass?" Joe stepped up to the slider, and something crunched under his feet.

He lifted his right foot and stirred the broken glass with the toe of his shoe. "What's this?"

"Joe." Hailey was bending over, her face close to the glass door. "Look."

He zeroed in on her fingertip and saw a square of glass cut out from the door near the handle. He whistled. "Looks like Joost's place has been burglarized."

He stuck his finger through the hole and was able to flick down the lock on the door. "How thoughtful. The thief locked up after himself."

"Maybe he was hoping Joost wouldn't notice, or maybe Joost is the one who locked it after he got home."

Hailey rapped on the glass and called out. "Joost? It's Hailey Duvall. Are you home?"

Joe cocked his head, listening for a response. Then he kicked the glass out of the way and said, "Nope, the burglars locked up after they did their business."

Joe had already unlocked the door from the inside, so he grabbed the handle to yank open the slider.

Hailey put her hand on his arm. "What are you doing?"

"I'm going to see what happened to Joost's place. If we're lucky, the thieves will still be here and I can get some answers out of them."

"Is that always your first response?" Hailey wedged one hand on her slim hip. "That's what motivated you to jump on that car this morning, too."

"Damn straight. You can't let the bastards get away when they're under your noses." He slipped his gun out of its holster and pulled open the door. When he stepped inside, he thought he'd made a wrong turn into a computer lab. Rows of monitors blinked at him, and others displayed scrolling data.

Hailey took a slow turn around the room. "I guess the burglars weren't after computer equipment."

Joe put a finger to his lips and crept toward the bathroom, the only other room in the apartment. When he saw it was empty, he returned to the other room, where Hailey was standing next to the door. He shook his head at her. "Nobody here."

"What were they after?" Hailey picked up an up-ended sofa cushion and dropped it. "Loose change?"

Joost's place was that of a bachelor—his living room doubled as his bedroom, and the large bed in the corner had been searched, its mattress askew, the covers ripped off and tossed aside.

Hailey traced her fingers down the spines of the books that had been pulled off the shelves and restacked, helter-skelter. Folding her arms over her chest, she turned toward him. "Are you thinking what I'm thinking?"

"That someone knew Marten was staying here and decided to look for his stuff?"

She nodded. "That about covers it."

"Then, yeah, we're on exactly the same page."

"Stop right where you are."

Joe spun around, stepping in front of Hailey and aiming his gun at the door. He stopped when he caught sight of the curly-haired blond wielding a baseball bat like Babe Ruth on steroids.

"Joost?" Hailey waved her arms. "I'm Hailey. This is my friend Joe. We just got here and saw that someone had broken into your place."

The Dutchman tightened his grip on the bat and then dropped it and rushed to the bank of computers, jabbering in what had to be Dutch.

Joe cleared his throat. "Doesn't look like those have been touched."

"I hope not. I have about a year's worth of work for this one customer cranking away on these computers."

"Your books, your bed, every other piece of furniture, however, suffered a good going-over." Hailey flung out one arm to encompass the disheveled room.

Joost pushed the curls from his eyes. "Good luck finding anything of value other than the computers."

Joe asked, "Is there anything missing? Can you even tell?"

Joost surveyed the mess. "The only thing I can think of is in the bathroom. Did they ransack the bathroom, too?"

"Couldn't tell at first glance. I just poked my head in there to make sure the thieves were gone."

The bat dragging on the floor behind him, Joost loped into the bathroom and threw open the mirrored door of the medicine cabinet. He spit out an expletive, which sounded a lot more expressive in Dutch.

"They took my meds."

"Your meds?" Hailey glanced at Joe and tapped her head.

"My medication. I suffer from what you'd call social anxiety. The drugs I take for that are in high demand on the black market."

"Oh, sorry." Hailey grimaced. "Can you get them replaced?"

"I'll call my doctor."

"What about the police? Are you going to call the police?" Joe folded his arms and wedged his shoulder against the bathroom's doorjamb.

"I have to if I want my doctor to give me refills. I think I have to submit a police report or something."

Hailey nudged Joe's back. "Is there anything else missing, Joost?"

"Not that I notice." Joost hunched his rounded shoulders. "I'm just glad they didn't touch the computers."

"Don't you think that's weird?" Joe stepped back as Joost made a move to leave the bathroom. "Thousands of dollars of computer equipment and the thief takes a couple bottles of pills?"

"He was probably a junkie. Didn't care about the computers, probably didn't have the means to move them out of here."

Joe pointed to the sliding glass door. "A junkie with burglary tools? That was a glass cutter."

"I don't know." Joost ran his hand over the top of one of his monitors in a caress. "I'll let the cops figure that out. It's not like they're going to catch him. The SFPD doesn't put much effort into catching petty criminals."

"If that's what he was." Hailey perched on the arm of a sofa covered in comic books, dumped there from the basket lying on its side next to a cushion from the same sofa.

"Why wouldn't he be?" Joost drew a pair of shaggy blond eyebrows over his nose.

Hailey tapped the toe of her boot. "Joost, we came here because you called me about Marten, told me he'd left something with you and had asked you to call me if he didn't return. Then Marten mysteriously disappears, nefarious types start looking for him and someone breaks into your place. You still think this was some junkie looking for a high?"

Joost's round face crinkled. "Marten disappeared mysteriously? He just left. He was here one day and the next day...gone. Those guys searching for him? Probably bookies. I grew up with Marten in The Hague. Marten was born mysterious, so nothing he does surprises me. Are you worried about him?"

Hailey placed her hands on her knees and hunched forward. "We were supposed to meet on the last ferry to Alcatraz yesterday. You heard the news about someone falling or jumping from an Alcatraz ferry?"

Joost nodded, his pale blue eyes wide.

"*That* ferry." Hailey compressed her lips into a thin line.

"You think that was Marten who went overboard? Last I heard it was a hoax and nobody went over."

"I thought I saw him on the ferry that night, and he—" she jerked her thumb at Joe "—followed Marten right onto the ferry, but he never came off and I haven't heard from him since."

Joost transferred his gaze from Hailey to Joe. "Why were you following Marten?"

Joe threw up his hands. "That doesn't matter. We think he was pushed off that boat...murdered."

"That wasn't Marten. He could've survived in the bay." Joost shook a finger at Hailey. "He was half a second away from making the Olympic swim team for the Netherlands. The coast guard hasn't found a body yet."

Joe preferred the angry, bat-wielding Joost to this mellow dude who had an explanation for everything.

Hailey pressed the heel of her hand to her forehead. "I don't know if Marten is dead or alive. I don't know what happened on that ferry, but there are too many strange coincidences going on, and now your place has been burglarized minutes before I get here, ready to collect Marten's things."

"Hours."

"Excuse me?"

"I've been gone since this morning. The break-in could've happened hours ago."

"Okay, whatever." Hailey rolled her eyes at Joe.

Joe took a deep breath. "We don't know what happened to Marten, but what we do know is that someone broke into your place and you don't even know if Marten's things were stolen. Have you looked? Was his stuff in this room?"

"Things?" Joost blinked his eyes. "Did I say 'things'? It's just one thing Marten left for you in case he didn't return, and that couldn't have been stolen."

"And why is that?" Joe gritted his teeth, feeling the last bit of his patience slip away.

Joost patted his chest. "Because I have it right here with me."

HAILEY SLID OFF the arm of the sofa and collapsed against the cushion, the comic books crinkling beneath her. "Why didn't you say that to begin with?"

"I didn't realize you were concerned about what Marten left for you."

"That's why we're here." Spreading her arms wide, Hailey kicked up her feet on the messy coffee table.

Joe held out his hand. "So, what did he leave her? A note?"

"No." Joost reached into his front pocket and withdrew something pinched between his fingers. He held it up, and it caught the light from the window and winked. "A key."

"A key?" Hailey swung her legs from the table and jumped up. "A key to what?"

"I don't know." Joost bounced the key in his palm before dumping it into Joe's outstretched hand.

As Joe studied the key, Hailey sidled next to him, her hair brushing his forearm.

"Why would he leave me a key without an explanation?"

"Maybe he was afraid it would fall into the wrong hands." Joe plucked up the key chain, a cardboard circle ringed with metal. "There's some writing on this."

Hailey squinted at the white circle as Joe held it up. "The letters are rubbed out. Looks like an *M, I, S...* Trust Marten to leave me a clue that needs another clue to figure it out."

"Born mysterious." Joost tapped the side of his nose. "That label had something written on it in pencil. I may have rubbed it off with a sweaty thumb, or maybe Marten did."

Joe ground his back teeth. "Did mysterious Marten tell you anything about this key, like maybe what it unlocked?"

"Marten told me nothing. He called last-minute, asked if he could crash at my place for a few days, didn't bring any luggage with him, and I barely saw him. Yesterday morning, he gave me that key and told me to give it to Hailey if he didn't return. He didn't return, and I called Hailey at the number he gave me." Joost held up his hands. "That's all I know. I'm sure Marten is fine. He has nine lives, like a cat."

"Cats don't swim." Hailey hitched her bag over her shoulder. "You have my number. Let me know if you happen to hear from Marten."

"At least you have the key." Joost had turned to face his precious computers, his duty to Marten done.

Joe dangled the key from its key chain. "Yeah, a key to nowhere for Miss Nobody."

"If I remember anything, I'll call you."

Joe snapped his fingers. "Did he tell you he also had a hotel room? Maybe that's why he didn't have any luggage with him."

"Didn't say anything about a hotel. Maybe he's holed up there to escape his gambling debts."

"Thanks, Joost." Hailey made a face at Joe and pointed to the sliding door with the square hole in the glass that Joost didn't seem very concerned about.

They stepped outside, and Hailey swung around to face him, her eyes throwing sparks. "Why would Marten leave me a key and not tell me what it's supposed to unlock?"

"Maybe the name on the key chain would've told

you if Joost hadn't rubbed it off with his sweaty thumb."

"I'm not sure about that. Really, when was the last time you ever referred to anyone as Miss? Most people, including Marten, use Ms."

Joe used Miss a lot, but he probably shouldn't let Hailey in on that. "Maybe it's like one of those schools, like Miss Watson's School for Wayward Boys."

Hailey punched him in the arm, and he tightened his bicep.

"Is that the one you went to?" She rubbed her knuckles.

"Close to it." He twisted his lips into a smile. "Are you ready to go home?"

"I'm ready to locate the owner of this key. What do you think Marten left for me?"

"Maybe the retraction of his statement to the CIA regarding Denver's involvement in the Syria bombing, or whatever it was he was going to tell you at your meeting. Sounds like he had a feeling he'd never make it to the meeting."

Hailey bit her bottom lip as she put a hand on his arm. "Would you mind coming back to my place with me? Maybe we can figure out this key thing together."

"I was going to suggest the same thing." He didn't mean to scare her to get the invitation, but that seemed to be the effect of his words.

"I'll order a car." She dug into her purse and pulled out her phone. "Looks like I missed a call from Agent Porter."

"Do you want to call him back while we wait for the car?"

"He left a voice mail." She tapped her phone and listened with the tip of her tongue lodged in the corner of her mouth. She shook her head at him and mouthed, "Nothing."

When she finished listening to the voice mail, she said, "The police found the stolen car abandoned in San Jose, no prints. Agent Porter put in a request for MI6 to look into the whereabouts of Andrew. That's all they have. No news on Marten."

"Are you going to tell Porter about the key Marten left you?"

"No. I have a feeling if I gave the key to him, it would disappear into the black hole of this noninvestigation." Her eyebrows formed a V over her nose. "Unless you think I should."

"They don't know what we know, and they don't believe what I believe. They're not going to take it as seriously as I do, but I'm not going to tell you *not* to contact them with what you have and suspect."

"Suspect." She skimmed a hand through her dark hair, somehow making messy look chic. "That's the key word, isn't it? I don't even have the video of Andrew tied to that chair." She covered her eyes with one hand. "Andrew asked me for help in that video, and I haven't been able to do a damn thing."

He put a tentative hand on her back. "That's not true. Porter just said MI6 is going to track down Andrew. You're doing everything you can, Hailey."

"I did try calling him, but there's no answer and no opportunity to leave a voice mail. I just wish I could do more."

"You can't save the world, even with all your father's money."

"I can give it a try." She pointed her phone up the street. "Our car is coming."

Twenty minutes later the car dropped them off on Pacific Avenue in front of Hailey's father's house.

Hailey trod up the stairs ahead of him, her steps heavy. Joe wanted to solve this mystery to clear Major Denver, but now he had another motive—to protect Hailey.

As they turned toward the last few steps to the porch, a woman rose from behind the bushes and raised a hand clutching a gun toward Hailey.

Joe's reflexes kicked into high gear. He threw himself between Hailey and the dark-haired woman, grabbing the woman's proffered hand and twisting it behind her back.

As the woman screamed, Hailey yelled behind him, "Joe, stop. That's Ayala."

Chapter Seven

Hailey grabbed a handful of Joe's jacket, trying to pull him off Ayala. Had he gone insane?

He stepped back, releasing his hold on her friend. "God, I'm so sorry. I thought you had a gun in your hand."

Ayala, her dark eyes wide and glassy, pointed to the rolled-up umbrella she'd dropped to the ground. "I-it's an umbrella."

"Are you all right? Did I hurt your arm?" Joe swept up the umbrella from the porch and handed it to Ayala.

Ayala smoothed one hand over her skirt, shooting a gaze at Hailey over Joe's broad shoulder. "I'm fine."

Hailey scooted around Joe and hugged the nurse. "I'm so sorry, Ayala. What are you doing here?"

"Heard you were having a fund-raiser. How could I miss it?" Her eyes shifted toward Joe as she folded her arms, clamping her umbrella to her chest.

"I thought you couldn't make it, but I'm glad you did. I sent you an email yesterday. Did you get it?"

"I'm sorry. I just have my cell phone with me, and

I hate reading emails on my phone. Wh-who's your friend?"

"Ayala, this is Joe McVie. Joe, this is Ayala Khan, the nurse who worked with me at the refugee camp."

Joe stuck out his hand. "Nice to meet you. I feel like an idiot."

Ayala's lips turned up in a quick smile as she clasped Joe's hand briefly with her own and then shoved hers in the pocket of her coat. "I'm fine, really, even though it's not the greeting I expected."

"Of course not." Hailey chuckled. "We're a little on edge here."

Joe poked Hailey in the back, and she straightened her shoulders. Did he think she was going to keep all of this from someone who could be in the direct line of fire? "Come on in, Ayala. How long have you been waiting out here and why didn't you call me?"

"It was all last-minute. I went home to Florida first, and I wanted to surprise you. I didn't realize what a stupid idea that was until I landed on your porch and you didn't answer the door."

"But you knew I'd be in town because of the gala." Hailey pushed open the front door and ushered Ayala inside while scowling at Joe.

He made his fingers into a gun and placed his index finger against his temple before scooping up Ayala's bags and following them into the house.

"Can I get you something to drink? Water? Juice? Tea?"

Ayala tilted her head back and spun around the room. "Wow, this is some place you have here."

"Full disclosure." Hailey held up two fingers. "Not mine."

"I know it's your father's. Still, it's a fancy place to crash." Ayala waved her hands. "Not that I'm crashing here. I was just getting ready to call a few hotels when you came home."

"Don't be ridiculous. The house is huge. I think I can find a spare bedroom or two for you to occupy."

"I don't want to—" Ayala nodded at Joe, who was stacking her bags in the corner of the room "—intrude."

"Joe's just a friend. He's staying at a hotel." She didn't even sound convincing to her own ears.

Joe finally finished his task, which he'd obviously drawn out to give her and Ayala a chance to talk, and brushed his hands together. "Did I hear my name? Not calling the cops on me, are you?"

"Oh, please. It's already forgotten." Ayala tipped her head to one side. "It's clear you were trying to protect Hailey. Does she need it?"

Hailey cleared her throat. "How about that tea?"

"Thanks. I'd like some." Ayala patted her purse. "I can also get on the phone to a hotel and book myself a room."

"Don't say another word about that. We'll work out a fair trade." Hailey flicked her fingers in Joe's direction. "Just ask Joe about that."

"Uh-oh. What am I getting myself into?" Ayala's gaze darted between her and Joe.

"You always speak so passionately on behalf of the refugees." Hailey made a move toward the kitchen and crooked her finger at Ayala. "I'm hoping you can give a speech at the fund-raiser. Nothing long, just a little recap of the work you do there."

Ayala trailed after her into the kitchen. "You mean the work *you* do. It's money from people like you and your guests that keep things moving there. Don't expect me to stand up and toot my own horn."

"Anything you want to say, just talk about the work that needs to be done to get them to open their wallets and checkbooks." Hailey reached into the cupboard for two cups and called into the other room, "Joe, would you like some tea?"

"I'm all tea-ed out, thanks."

Ayala sidled up next to Hailey at the counter and nudged her with a sharp elbow. "If he's not taken, do you mind if I try my luck? He's hot."

"Oh." Speaking of hot, Hailey's cheeks flamed. "Y-you— Sure, if you want."

Ayala raised one dark brow. "So that's how it is. You're not fooling me, Hailey Duvall. You might be calling him a friend today, but you want more tomorrow. Am I right?"

"Well, you said it." Hailey winked. "He *is* hot."

"Where and how did you meet him? Is he military?"

"How'd you guess that?" Hailey shoved the tea-kettle beneath the faucet and filled it half-full.

"The way he carries himself, his clipped manner of speaking. Don't forget, I've been around plenty of American servicemen."

"He's Delta Force."

Ayala's eyes flickered.

Did she remember that Major Denver was Delta Force?

"Is he someone you met in Syria?"

"No." Hailey cranked on the burner and then turned to face Ayala, taking her arm. "We'll explain every-thing to you—together. It's been a crazy few days, and I can't tell you how happy I am to see you here."

Joe straddled a stool at the center island in the kitchen. "Maybe Ayala wants to freshen up a little."

"Great idea." Ayala drummed her fingers on the counter as she swept out of the kitchen.

Hailey hissed. "That was rude. What was that about?"

"Do you really think we should tell her everything that's been going on?"

"Why not? She's involved in it as much as I am—more, as she's still working at the refugee camp."

"Giving her knowledge could put her in danger."

Hailey jumped as the kettle whistled. She grabbed the handle and poured the boiling water over the tea bags in the two cups. "The way I see it, she's already in danger, Joe. Telling her everything just might give her a chance to stay safe. If anything happened to her and I had neglected to give her the 411 about Marten and Andrew, I'd never forgive myself."

Ayala suddenly appeared at the entrance to the kitchen. "Oh, no. Hailey has a hard time forgiving herself for a lot of imagined infractions. I wouldn't want to pile on." She perched on the stool next to Joe's, crossing one leg over the other and swinging it back and forth. "You'd better tell me everything."

Hailey placed a cup in front of Ayala. "It all started with a call from Marten de Becker."

Hailey told Ayala about everything that had gone on the past few days—except that she'd become dependent on Joe McVie as her savior and bodyguard. Ayala had already figured that out anyway.

As Hailey came to the end of her story, she fished Marten's key from the front pocket of her jeans and slid it across the counter. "Here's the key Marten's friend gave me, but I have no idea what it unlocks. Any ideas?"

Ayala picked up the key and turned it over, running her thumb over the cardboard key chain. "Mis? Could it be someone's name?"

Joe spoke up. "That's what I thought."

"It looks old." Ayala bounced the key in the palm of her hand. "What could Marten have been into? This could all just be about his shady lifestyle, his gambling, his women."

"Maybe, but what about the video of Andrew?"

Ayala shivered and tipped her hand over, dropping the key on the counter. "That's horrible. The only thing

I have going for me is that I never ID'd Major Rex Denver as one of the men who held us, and I'm not writing an article about the incident."

"Is that what Andrew is doing?" Hailey wrapped her hands around the cup, warming them. "That's probably why these guys got to him. They probably don't want any further attention focused on the bombing in case Andrew brings more information to light about Denver."

"Then why you?" Ayala touched Hailey's hand. "All you did was bring up the fact that one of our kidnappers spoke French with an American accent and someone called him Denver, which I completely missed. You aren't changing that story…are you?"

"I have no reason to change it."

Joe folded his hands together and hunched forward on the counter, resting on his forearms. "We're beginning to think the people involved are tracking Hailey because Marten reached out to her—or tried to reach out to her."

"Then maybe you should just forget about Marten, Hailey. I know that sounds callous, but you can't help him now." Ayala traced the edge of the key on the counter. "Toss this out and forget about everything. If someone is framing Major Denver, let the US Army figure it out." She shot a quick glance at Joe. "Sorry."

"No need to apologize to me." Joe rubbed his knuckles across the stubble on his chin. "I agree with you. The US Army needs to be doing everything in its power to investigate the matter as a setup, and there's more and more evidence leaking out that it was a setup."

"Where *is* Denver?" Ayala raised her cup to her lips, her dark eyes watching Joe over the rim.

"Nobody knows. He went AWOL after a meeting he'd arranged with an informant went south."

"In Afghanistan?"

"Yes."

Ayala carefully wiped her lipstick from the cup with the edge of her thumb. "Maybe he's already dead."

"I don't believe that." Joe's hands curled into fists against the granite.

"Again, I'm sorry. I know you're concerned about your Delta Force commander, but I'm concerned about my friend."

"I'm concerned about Hailey, too. I don't want her mixed up with this, and I'm not expecting her to go to bat for Denver."

Hailey waved. "Hello. I'm standing right here. Neither one of you needs to be worried about me. And I'm not going to forget about Marten, Andrew, Denver or any of them."

Joe's and Ayala's eyes met, and they said in unison, "Do-gooder."

"Now you're ganging up on me, but I'm serious." She put her cup in the sink and turned toward Ayala. "Do you want more tea, or would you like to get settled in a room upstairs?"

"If you're sure I'm not putting you out."

"Are you prepared to say a few words at the fund-raiser?" Hailey held her breath. Ayala could be such an asset at this event, but she was shy.

"I'd be happy to talk *briefly*."

Hailey clapped her hands. "Then make yourself at home."

"I'm going to get back to my hotel." Joe straightened up and stretched, and Hailey tried not to stare at the way his shirt molded to his chest, although Ayala didn't seem to have the same reservations.

"It was nice to meet you, Joe, and thanks for looking out for my friend." Ayala draped an arm around Hailey's shoulders.

"I'm glad she has company here." Joe grabbed his jacket. "Can I take you ladies out to dinner tonight?"

"Of course." Hailey wrapped one arm around Ayala's waist to make sure her friend knew she wouldn't be intruding. "We'd love dinner."

"I don't—" Ayala jumped when Hailey pinched her side. "Sounds good to me."

Ayala extricated herself from Hailey and headed for her bags in the corner. "I'm going to pick out a room now."

"Stick to the first two on the right. They share a connected bathroom. Clean towels in the cupboard."

"Just like a hotel but better." Ayala hitched her carry-on bag over her shoulder. "See you later, Joe."

"See you." Joe peeked around the corner of the kitchen to watch Ayala go up the stairs and then joined Hailey at the sink. "Speaking of hotels, I think it's worth it to check out Marten's."

"Do you think he still has a room there?" Hailey reached around Joe's solid form to pick up Ayala's cup.

"Why wouldn't he? I told you, I picked up Marten's trail from the Pacific Rim Hotel, not from some house in the Sunset District. He went straight to the ferry from the hotel. If he never returned, he never checked out."

The cup slipped from Hailey's fingers and clattered in the sink as it broke in two pieces. "You didn't tell me it was the Pacific Rim."

Joe sucked in a breath. "Did you cut yourself?"

"No." Hailey held up her hand. "The Pacific Rim, are you sure?"

"Yeah, fancy digs. If Marten was gambling, he must've had a good run."

"That's where my fund-raiser is going to be." She picked up the broken teacup by the handle and dropped it into the trash. "I wonder if Marten knew that."

"If he did, why wouldn't he just set up a meeting at the hotel?" Joe pinched the other piece of the cup between his thumb and forefinger and threw it away. "If you're having the fund-raiser there, do you think you can get access to Marten's room?"

"Don't worry. I can get access to Marten's room, no problem."

"Do you know a manager at the hotel?"

"Better than that. I know the owner—it's my father."

JOE ADJUSTED THE scarf around his neck and turned his back to the wind as it whipped around the corner of his hotel. He'd rather be having dinner with Hailey alone tonight, but with Ayala in town he now had a package deal.

Hadn't his fortune at lunch today encouraged him to take a chance on a dark-haired beauty? Ayala had dark hair and beauty to spare, but he had eyes for just one brunette. He'd already taken a chance on a blonde and failed. Would hair color make a difference?

A sleek white Jag pulled up to the hotel's loading zone, and the passenger window buzzed down. Hailey leaned over the seat and called out the window. "Hey, stranger, need a ride?"

Joe slid into the car and onto the warm leather seat. "Never thought I'd appreciate a seat warmer, but that wind off the bay cuts right to your bones."

Ayala leaned forward from the back seat. "Can you imagine how I feel coming from Florida?"

"Yeah, don't knock the seat warmers." Hailey skimmed her hands over the steering wheel. "Where are we having dinner?"

"I made reservations at a steak house in the Financial District—Jackson's on Jackson. Is that okay?"

"Good choice. You must've read the reviews." Hailey pulled out of the hotel and into traffic.

Joe twisted his head around. "Is that okay with you, Ayala? If you don't eat steak, they have fish and even some vegetarian entrées."

"Steak is fine by me."

It didn't take long for Hailey to navigate the traffic,

and twenty minutes later she was handing her keys to a valet attendant.

They took an elevator up to the top floor of the office building, where the restaurant commanded a view over the glittering lights of the city and the Transamerica Building formed a triangle in the sky.

Would've been a romantic spot if not for the third wheel. Joe pulled out Hailey's chair and then made a grab for Ayala's chair. He'd already twisted the woman's arm behind her back; he didn't want her to know his real thoughts.

She smiled her thanks and took her seat as a waiter scurried over to deliver water and a basket of bread.

Hailey sighed. "This is nice."

Ayala raised her water glass to her lips and gazed over the rim at the view. "A long way from Syria, isn't it?"

Joe asked, "Are you going back soon or staying in Florida for a while?"

"Just two weeks in Florida before returning to the refugee camp."

"It must get—" Joe waved a piece of bread in the air "—depressing. How long have you been doing the work?"

"For a few years now. It's not depressing to me. Those are my people, you know. My parents immigrated to the US from Syria. I have an older brother who was born there. I'd been working as a nurse, and as soon as I learned about the need for medical care during the civil war, I knew I had to help."

Joe bowed his head. "I am humbled to be in the presence of two such selfless, generous people."

"As Delta Force, you do your part, too—just in a different way." Hailey opened the wine menu. "Should we share a bottle?"

"I'm not much of a wine drinker, but you two go ahead. I'm a beer guy—you can take the boy out of Southie, but you can't take the Southie out of the boy."

Ayala shook her head. "All I can handle is one glass, Hailey, so unless you're prepared to polish off that bottle yourself, we should probably stick to single drinks."

"You've been in Syria too long. You used to be able to drink us under the table." Hailey wrinkled her nose. "But if you're opting out, I'm not going to order a whole bottle for myself."

The waiter approached their table. "Can I get you something to drink?"

Hailey ordered a glass of cabernet, Ayala ordered a martini and Joe stuck with a beer.

When the waiter left, Joe offered the basket of bread to Ayala. "Tell me about your experiences in Syria. Think of it as prep for the speech you owe Hailey."

Ayala waved off the bread. "I've been working out there for about three years. While I was at a symposium in Florida on emergency room treatments, I—I ran into a few nurses who had been working at some of the refugee centers. The work sounded incredible and I was stuck in a rut, so it was perfect timing for me."

"And for them." Hailey ran a fingertip up the outside of her water glass. "The need couldn't be greater right now."

"It's so dangerous, though, as you both found out. Do you feel safe there, Ayala?"

"Most of the time. What happened to us—" she glanced at Hailey from beneath her eyelashes "—that was an aberration. A onetime thing."

"I know it put a damper on the peace negotiations. Have both sides recovered from the damage that bombing caused?"

The waiter appeared with their drinks, and Ayala sank back in her seat and took a long pull from her martini glass before he and Hailey even had their drinks in front of them. He'd have to steer the conversation in another direction. Either the violence bothered Ayala more than she let on, or she didn't want to talk business tonight.

Once they ordered their food and all had their drinks in hand, Hailey raised her glass. "To my bodyguard and keynote speaker and a successful fundraiser."

They clinked glasses and Ayala took another big sip of her drink. "Keynote? I'm saying a few words, right?"

"As many or as few as you like." Hailey swirled the ruby wine in her glass. "I think I mentioned already that our keynote speaker is Dr. Nabil Karam-Thomas. You remember. He visited us at the refugee center."

Ayala raised her napkin to her face, covering the

lower half. "I—I do remember. He's much more elo-
quent than I am."

"You don't have to speak at all if you don't want
to, Ayala. I was joking about earning your keep at
the house."

"I know you were, and I really don't mind talking.
I just don't like going into the graphic details or the
political landscape."

Was that directed at him? He'd definitely be changing the topic, but if he were involved in such a selfless
endeavor, he'd want to tell everyone about it. Maybe
Ayala thought he was trying to glean information from
her about Denver. At the house, Ayala had suggested
Hailey stay as far away from the inquiries into Denver's
involvement in the bombing as possible, and it seemed
as if she were taking her own advice.

Joe took a sip of beer through the thick head of
foam. "Where do you live in Florida, Ayala?"

Ayala preferred talking about Florida to Syria and
seemed to finally open up and lose her reserve—or
maybe that apple martini she'd been guzzling had
something to do with it.

When the food arrived, both women ordered a second round of drinks while Joe nursed his beer. Someone would have to drive home.

Hailey tapped Ayala's empty martini glass. "Looks
like we could've finished that bottle of wine together."

"Oh, this?" Ayala pinged her glass. "It's sour apple.
It doesn't taste like alcohol at all."

Hailey rolled her eyes. "Like I said before, you've

been in Syria too long. Those are the most dangerous kinds of drinks. Right, Joe?"

"I wouldn't know." He curled his fingers around the handle of his mug. "I'm a beer guy."

By the end of dinner, Joe knew a lot about Florida and San Francisco but very little about the two women who lived in those cities. Ayala kept her conversation surface level, and while Joe wanted to know more about Hailey, he didn't want to make those discoveries with an audience.

Ayala excused herself to use the ladies' room, and she hadn't been joking about being a lightweight. As she rose from her chair, she staggered and grabbed the edge of the table to steady herself.

"Are you all right?" Hailey put a hand on Ayala's arm.

"I'm fine. Just got up too fast."

Hailey watched her friend as she wended her way through the tables in the dining room. Then she rested her elbow on the table and buried her chin in her hand. "Thank you."

"For what? Dinner?" He fingered the check the waiter had placed discreetly at his elbow. "I haven't paid for it yet."

She cracked a smile. "Oh, that, too, but I'm thanking you for engaging Ayala in conversation. I've never heard her so animated and open."

"That was open?"

"For her it was. She's very reserved and has gotten even more so the longer she spends at the refugee center."

"Sounds like she might need a break."

"I know I did after…" Hailey drained her glass, and her lips in the candlelight appeared stained red with wine.

"Are you going to be okay to drive home?"

"Probably not." She twisted her head to the side. "Where's Ayala?"

"She's *definitely* not okay to drive. I'm glad one of us stayed sober." Joe slipped his wallet from his pocket and slid a credit card onto the tray.

The waiter picked up the check and the empty glasses and asked them if they wanted anything else—twice—before Hailey pushed back from the table. "I'd better check on Ayala. She's been in there long enough to wash her hair in the sink."

As she walked away from the table, Joe called after her, "Be careful."

Or maybe she just imagined his warning. Why should she be careful on her way to the ladies' room in a restaurant? Regardless, a little chill caused a rash of goose bumps to race across her arms. She rubbed them and headed toward the bar.

She hesitated at the entrance to the dim hallway that led to the restrooms and an emergency exit. A man brushed past her, and she jumped. Hailey straightened her spine and marched to the ladies' room.

She pushed open the door and poked her head inside. "Ayala?"

A woman washing her hands at the sink met Hailey's eyes in the mirror and then looked away.

Hailey took two steps into the bathroom, which contained three stalls. The doors to two of the stalls yawned open. Hailey rapped her knuckles against the closed third door. "Ayala?"

The woman at the sink plucked a paper towel from a stack on the sink. "That stall was occupied when I walked in, but I haven't heard anyone in there."

The doors to the stalls reached the floor, so Hailey couldn't peek beneath. With her head pounding, she knocked on the door again. "Ayala?"

This time, a soft moan answered her and Hailey gasped. "Did you hear that?"

"I did." The woman was literally clutching her pearls. "Should we call the manager?"

"Go, go." Hailey shoved into the stall next to the locked one and climbed onto the toilet seat. She peered over the top and yelped. "Oh my God. My friend's passed out."

Hailey managed to clamber over the top of the separator between the two stalls and opened the door before crouching next to Ayala.

Another woman stood in front of the stall, gaping. "What happened?"

"My friend's ill. I think someone went to get the manager. Can you call 911?"

"Of course."

Hailey curled her arm beneath Ayala's head. "Ayala. Ayala, what's wrong? What happened?"

Her friend groaned as white foam bubbled from her lips. "Help me. I've been poisoned."

Chapter Eight

The woman who'd left to get the manager stumbled back into the bathroom. "Is she okay? I called 911."

Hailey peeled her tongue from the roof of her dry mouth. "She lost consciousness. Can you sit with her for a minute while I get my friend? What's your name?"

"Marcia." The woman knelt beside Hailey and put her hand on Ayala's forehead. "She's clammy."

"I'll be right back." Hailey charged out of the bathroom and emerged from the hallway into the dining area.

Joe must've been watching for her. He immediately jumped up from the table and strode to her side. "What's wrong?"

"It's Ayala. She's been poisoned."

Cursing, Joe charged past her to the restroom. "Is she in the ladies' room?"

"She's in the last stall."

"Conscious?"

"Barely. Someone already called 911."

"Good." Joe pushed into the ladies' room and crouched next to Marcia.

"Thank you." Hailey put a hand on Marcia's back. "How's she doing?"

"Still unconscious, but her pulse is strong…and the foaming has stopped."

Joe looked up from his assessment of Ayala. "She was foaming at the mouth?"

"A little when I first found her." Hailey helped Marcia to her feet. "Could I ask you for one more favor? Could you please tell the manager that there's an impaired woman in the restroom and that 911 is on the way? I don't think that other woman ever alerted the manager."

"Absolutely. I hope she's going to be all right. I've seen a lot of people passed out from booze, but not with foam coming out of their mouths." Marcia backed out of the bathroom.

Hailey dropped to the floor next to Joe, who'd rolled up his jacket and shoved it beneath Ayala's head.

"What the hell happened?" His harsh whisper echoed in the empty bathroom.

"When I came in here to look for Ayala, there was a woman at the sink and a locked stall. I called Ayala's name at the door of the stall, but she didn't answer. The woman at the sink told me the stall had been locked when she came into the bathroom. I banged on the door and heard a groan."

"Was it Marcia at the sink?"

"No, that woman took off. Marcia came in later."

Hailey broke off as someone barreled through the bathroom door.

The manager poked his head in the stall. "Is she all right?"

Joe pressed two fingers against Ayala's neck. "She's still alive but unconscious. Are the paramedics here yet?"

"Not yet, although I saw them arrive street level."

"Could you do me a favor and keep everyone out of here, and when the paramedics arrive, guide them in here? Let them know the woman mentioned poisoning before she lost consciousness."

The manager jerked back. "Poisoning? Not in my restaurant. More like alcohol poisoning."

"Just let them know that's what she mentioned. It might be helpful when they treat her." Joe tipped his chin toward Hailey when the manager swept out of the bathroom.

"That's what she told you, right?"

"Yes. When she wouldn't respond or open the door, I climbed onto the toilet seat in the stall next to hers, saw her slumped on the floor and hoisted myself over the top. She was mumbling and foam or spittle was forming at the corners of her mouth. When I got down next to her, she said she'd been poisoned, and then she passed out. I asked Marcia to get the manager and call 911, and then I ran out to get you."

"How could her food or drink have been poisoned here? Maybe it happened before she got to your place?"

"I don't know. If it was here, someone followed us. Were you watching out again?"

"Always. I'm always watching out." Joe put his finger to his lips as the paramedics burst through the bathroom door.

Hailey told them as much as she knew about Ayala's condition, and they took over.

An hour later, Hailey collected her keys from the valet and Joe held out his hand.

"I think I've completely sobered up by now, Joe."

"If you're sure. It might be better if you drive, anyway."

"Why is that?"

"Because you know how to get to the Pacific Rim Hotel."

She curled her hand around her keys until they bit into her flesh. "You want to look for Marten's room now?"

"I think it's past time. These people are getting bold...or desperate, and we need to put a stop to them." He opened the driver's-side door for her and she slid onto the seat.

She didn't even need the seat warmers. Joe's presence made her feel warm and secure, but she wanted to match his decisiveness. She couldn't depend on him forever.

"I'm going to call Agent Porter tomorrow and tell him what happened to Ayala."

"We don't know what happened to her yet."

"Just another attack on one of the kidnap victims

in Syria. They have to pay attention now. They have to take it seriously—Marten, Andrew, me and now Ayala. How much more proof do they need?"

"They need actual proof, not suspicions and supposition—Marten's body never turned up and nobody has reported him missing, we haven't heard anything back about Andrew, and we don't have the video. The attack on you could've been a wayward driver, and if Ayala *was* poisoned... I guess we'll see."

"Yeah, details, details." She swung out of the hotel's parking lot. "Let's see if Marten's room can offer us any proof."

The Pacific Rim was a hop and skip from the restaurant, but a car couldn't hop and skip through the San Francisco traffic. On the way over, Hailey tossed her phone into Joe's lap. "Can you please call the hospital where they took Ayala? It's San Francisco General."

Joe got the number from information, which then connected him to the hospital. He kept the phone and asked about Ayala.

"We're the ones who were with her. She's visiting from Florida. She doesn't have family here." He rolled his eyes at Hailey. "I'm on hold."

"Mention my father's name."

"What?"

"He raises a ton of money for that hospital."

Joe pressed his lips into a thin line, and Hailey's eyelid twitched. She sounded as bad as her father on one of his worst days—throwing around his weight and money. But this was for a good cause.

"I understand. Just a minute, please." He held out the phone to Hailey. "You're the expert. I wouldn't even know how to begin using that leverage."

Hailey swallowed and took the phone from him. "Yes, hello. This is Hailey Duvall. My father, Ray Duvall, helped fund the burn unit there at the hospital. Ayala Khan is my friend. She was visiting me and we were out to dinner when she became ill. I'd appreciate any information you could give me about her condition."

In her haste to give Hailey whatever she wanted, the nurse sputtered and stammered but was able to communicate that Ayala was doing well, had regained consciousness and would be ready to receive visitors tomorrow morning.

"Thank you so much. What's your name?"

"Shailene Franklin."

"Thanks, Shailene. I'll make sure to tell my father what great employees work at San Fran Gen the next time he meets with Mr. Sharpe, the director of operations."

Hailey ended the call and dropped her phone in the cup holder, ignoring Joe's gaze burning into the side of her face like a laser.

After several seconds, Joe cleared his throat. "Wow, so that's how it's done."

Hailey was thankful for the darkness of the car's

"FAST FIVE" READER SURVEY

Your participation entitles you to:
* 4 Thank-You Gifts Worth Over $20!

Complete the survey in minutes.

Get 2 FREE Books

Your Thank-You Gifts include **2 FREE BOOKS** and **2 MYSTERY GIFTS**. There's no obligation to purchase anything!

See inside for details.

Dear Reader,

Since you are a lover of our books, your opinions are important to us... and so is your time.

That's why we made sure your **"FAST FIVE" READER SURVEY** can be completed in just a few minutes. Your answers to the five questions will help us remain at the forefront of women's fiction.

And, as a thank-you for participating, we'd like to send you **4 FREE THANK-YOU GIFTS!**

Enjoy your gifts with our appreciation,

Pam Powers

To get your
4 FREE THANK-YOU GIFTS:

✳ Quickly complete the "Fast Five" Reader Survey
and return the insert.

"FAST FIVE" READER SURVEY

1 Do you sometimes read a book a second or third time? ○ Yes ○ No

2 Do you often choose reading over other forms of entertainment such as television? ○ Yes ○ No

3 When you were a child, did someone regularly read aloud to you? ○ Yes ○ No

4 Do you sometimes take a book with you when you travel outside the home? ○ Yes ○ No

5 In addition to books, do you regularly read newspapers and magazines? ○ Yes ○ No

YES! I have completed the above Reader Survey. Please send me my 4 FREE GIFTS (gifts worth over $20 retail). I understand that I am under no obligation to buy anything, as explained on the back of this card.

❑ I prefer the regular-print edition
182/382 HDL GM34

❑ I prefer the larger-print edition
199/399 HDL GM34

FIRST NAME | LAST NAME

ADDRESS

APT.# | CITY

STATE/PROV. | ZIP/POSTAL CODE

READER SERVICE—Here's how it works:

interior, which hid the warm blush on her cheeks. "I learned from the best."

"You keep saying that, and yet you seem to scorn *the best*, as you call your father."

Her hands tightened on the steering wheel. "What are you saying, Joe?"

He flashed his palm at her. "Look, I'm not criticizing you for using your father's name and influence to get what you want."

"Need."

"What?"

"To get what I need, not what I want."

"Okay, okay. I'd do the same. Anyone would, but you seem to heap scorn on your father for supplying you with the means to use his influence and money. It's kinda…"

"Hypocritical?"

His hand inched over to her thigh, and he skimmed his knuckles across the denim of her jeans. "You know what? You can just ignore me and my stupid judgments. I'm probably just jealous that the only string my pop could pull for me was for a free brewski at the corner tavern."

His apology felt as warm as his hand on her knee—heartfelt, sincere. Apologies flowed from his lips freely, as if he were accustomed to making them. What would Joe McVie have to apologize for in his life? Seemed as if he'd soldiered through a rough childhood and then made his way onto an elite military unit. He had loyalty and protectiveness—and muscles—to spare. He had no reason to be apologetic about anything, especially criticizing a spoiled rich girl.

She shrugged her shoulders with a quick lift and drop. "You don't have to apologize for expressing your honest opinion, but you can bask in the knowledge that you're running with someone with some different connections from your father—although you should never knock a free brewski."

He squeezed her knee before releasing it. "How'd you get to be such a guy's girl?"

"I'll give credit to my father for that, too. He raised me to take over his business."

"Not your brother?"

"I'm older." She pressed a hand to her chest. "And more responsible. Dad groomed me to handle the family business, until..."

"Until what?"

"There's the hotel. I'm going to swing around for the valet."

Joe whistled through his teeth. "Nice. How the hell did Marten afford this, and why would he want to stay in that hovel with Joost when he had a room waiting for him here?"

"I don't know. Maybe just to leave him that rusty old key to give me." She pulled up to the curb and stepped out when the attendant opened her door.

"Good evening, Ms. Duvall."

She peered at the valet's name tag. "Hello, Henry. How are you doing tonight?"

"Just fine, ma'am. I'll take good care of your car."

"You'd better." She winked at him. "It's my father's."

Joe placed a hand on her back and steered her through the front door. Leaning his head toward hers, he said, "How is this going to go down? Are you just going to tell them you want to get into Marten's room?"

"Pretty much." Hailey squared her shoulders and marched up to reception. She may have learned at her father's knee, but she could never master his full command over any and all situations. Hailey parked herself at the corner of the front desk while two clerks handled guests.

One of them looked up from her keyboard and smiled at Hailey. "I'll be right with you, miss. If you need the concierge, the desk is behind you, to your left."

Hailey opened her mouth to respond that she'd wait, but before she uttered one syllable, Timothy Tang, one of the night managers, came bustling from the back.

"Carmen, this is Ms. Duvall."

Two red spots exploded on Carmen's cheeks. "Oh, I'm sorry, Ms. Duvall."

Hailey waved her off. "Please. I wanted to speak to Mr. Tang, anyway."

The manager walked to the front desk, straightening the collar of his impeccable jacket. "What can I help you with, Ms. Duvall?"

"A friend of mine, Marten de Becker, has a room here but got called away to a business meeting in Sacramento for a day or two. He asked me to get something from his room, and I was wondering if you could let me in."

Mr. Tang's eye twitched for just a second, and then he said, "Of course. Let me check Mr. de Becker's room number."

"Thank you so much."

As Mr. Tang tapped on the keyboard, he asked, "Is everything going as planned for the gala? Gretchen has been working mostly with Josie, the event planner, but I've had an opportunity to make a few small contributions."

"Gretchen is really happy with how everything is working out." Hailey shot a glance at Joe, who was tapping his toe, arms crossed.

He said he wasn't going to judge.

"How do you like being night manager, Mr. Tang? Are you interested in event planning?"

"Oh." Mr. Tang met her gaze over the top of the monitor. "Josie is quite good at what she does, although I do like to chime in here and there—and I think she appreciates it."

"I'm sure she does."

"Seventh floor, room 728. That's Mr. de Becker's room." Mr. Tang slid a key card across the counter, his hand covering it until the last minute when Hailey snatched it up. "You can just drop the key off in any key receptacle on your way out, Ms. Duvall."

"I will do that. Thanks again, and I look forward to seeing you in a few nights."

Mr. Tang nodded quickly and then turned on his heel and disappeared into the back.

Turning toward Joe, Hailey plunged her hands in the pockets of her jacket, her fingers tracing the edges of the key card. "That wasn't bad."

Joe clapped his hands slowly three times as they veered toward the bank of elevators. "I'm in awe. I can't imagine your father, or anyone else, doing it better."

She snorted. "My father would have Mr. Tang thinking it was his idea and thanking him for the pleasure of serving him."

"You weren't too far off the mark." Joe thumbed the call button for the elevator. He ushered her in first when the doors opened. "Do all the employees have pictures of your family taped to their computer screens or something? They're all supposed to recognize you?"

"I wouldn't put it past my father to require that, but I don't care." She tugged on his sleeve. "You believe that, right? I don't care about that stuff."

"If you did, you wouldn't be running off to war-torn countries like Syria."

Hailey let out a little puff of breath. "My brother, on the other hand."

"Likes the perks, does he?"

"Revels in them. At first he just reveled in the money—drugs, booze, parties, women. Then when he realized that I had fallen out of favor with Dad, he began to clean up his act to suck up to him. Now he's his lapdog."

"How did you fall out of favor with your father?"

"Oh, this and that." She flicked her fingers.

Joe quirked one eyebrow. "So, your brother's in line to take over the family's holdings now?"

"Some, not all. Our father still doesn't trust him."

"Like he still trusts you."

"Sort of."

The elevator pinged and settled on the seventh floor. The thick carpet swallowed their footsteps as they made their way along the hallway to Marten's room.

When they reached his door, Hailey stuck the card in the slot and slid it out again. The green lights signaled entry, and Joe pushed open the door.

Entering the dark room on tiptoes, Hailey crossed her arms over her chest. She whispered, "Marten?"

Joe stabbed at the light switch on the wall by the door, and two lamps lit up the recesses of the big room.

Hailey scanned the area, nodding toward a suitcase in the corner. "His stuff. No wonder he didn't bring anything to Joost's place. He had it all here."

"Except for the key."

A chill skittered down her spine and Hailey made a half turn toward the door. "Lock it."

Joe flipped the latch at the top of the door to block entry from the outside.

Hailey pulled Marten's key from her purse. "Could it be a luggage lock?"

"I think it's too big, but give it a try." Joe made a move before she could and crossed the room to hoist Marten's single suitcase onto the king-size bed. He grabbed the zipper and pulled it across. "His bag isn't locked and doesn't even have a lock on it."

Hailey squeezed past him and flicked on the lights over the bed. "Maybe whatever this key unlocks is inside the suitcase."

"Maybe." Joe plunged his hands inside the suitcase, burying them in Marten's clothes.

Hailey reached past him and grabbed a fistful of shirts. "I don't think we have to worry about disturbing his things."

They pawed through the contents of Marten's suitcase, spreading shirts and pants across the bed.

Joe patted the outside pockets of the bag. "We're probably not going to find anything in his clothes."

Hailey let Joe search the zippered side pockets while she surveyed the room, hands on her hips. "Where's his laptop? I'm pretty sure Marten never went anywhere without it."

"Is there a safe?"

Hailey crossed to the cabinet beneath the TV. "It's in here."

Crouching in front of the cabinet, she threw open the doors. The safe gaped open, completely empty. "That's weird. Nothing in the safe—no passport, no money, no laptop."

Joe knelt beside her with socks clutched in his

hands. "Nothing in those side pockets, either, except these."

"Bathroom?" She bumped Joe's solid shoulder with her own.

He rose to his feet, extending a hand for her. She took it and he helped her to her feet. He didn't let go as he led her to the bathroom—and she didn't want him to.

The housekeeping staff had cleaned up since Marten's last day in the room. Clean towels towered on a rack, and fresh bottles of hotel toiletries lined the vanity.

"You'd think housekeeping would be curious as to the guest's whereabouts."

"As long as his departure date hasn't come and gone, I don't think they care or pay attention." She grabbed the handle of the bathroom door and pulled the door forward.

Marten's toiletry bag banged against the door.

Joe snatched it off the hook and dumped the contents on the counter of the sink.

The usual suspects rolled and spilled from the bag—shaving cream, razor, comb, condoms.

Hailey pinched a foil pack between her fingers. "Typical Marten. Wouldn't leave home without a stash of condoms."

"At least he played it safe in *some* areas of his life."

Hailey sank to the edge of the tub. "There's nothing

here. Nothing. Why did he want me to have that key? How am I supposed to figure out what it matches?"

"Come on. Let's get his clothes back in the suitcase." Joe shoveled Marten's toiletries into the bag and hung it back on the hook on the door.

Placing her palms against the cool porcelain of the tub, Hailey pushed up. "I'm disappointed. I was so proud of myself that I got us in here, and it all came to nothing."

"We didn't check all the drawers in the room. Maybe he stayed at this hotel because he knew you could get in here, and he left a note for you." Joe backed out of the bathroom.

"Why didn't he just leave a note with the key? Better yet, just leave me a note telling me what he was going to reveal to me on the ferry?"

"All of that would be too easy for someone else to find. He's obviously protecting this information." Joe crossed the room to the desk by the window and yanked open the top drawer.

Hailey placed one knee on the bed and plucked up one of Marten's shirts. As she folded it, a thump outside the door caused her to clutch the shirt to her chest.

"What was that?"

Joe squinted at her over the top of a piece of hotel stationery. "Maybe just housekeeping."

Hailey dropped the shirt and tiptoed to the door.

Placing one hand against the solid wood, she leaned forward and put her eye to the peephole.

She jerked back, her eyebrows colliding over her nose.

"Someone out there?" Joe crept up behind her.

"I can't see out the peephole. It's blocked or something."

Joe drew up beside her and nudged her over. "Let me have a look."

He peered through the peephole and immediately reared back, jamming his thumb against the peephole.

Hailey swallowed. "What's wrong?"

"Someone replaced the peephole with a camera. We're being watched."

Chapter Nine

Hailey staggered back from the door. "Are you serious?"

"Deadly." Keeping his finger against the door, Joe reached for the front pocket of his jeans. He pulled out a knife. "Open this for me."

With shaky fingers, Hailey pulled out the blade and handed the knife back to Joe. "What are you going to do?"

"Get rid of it." He slid his thumb from the peephole and held his hand cupped over it instead while he worked the point of the blade around the edge. After several minutes, he dug the device out of the door and closed his fist around it.

Tipping the back of her head against the wall, Hailey asked, "Someone was watching us this whole time?"

"Someone has had their eye on this room for who knows how long. That camera could've been there when Marten was still here."

"And after he…left—" Hailey licked her lips "—they

wanted to see who came in here. They must've already searched this room. Maybe they took his laptop. Where else would it be? He didn't leave it at Joost's place."

"Hailey, I'd love to stay here in this comfortable room talking to you all night, but we've gotta get out of here. The person or persons on the other side of this camera could be on their way right now."

A stream of adrenaline rushed through her body so fast it made her head hurt, and she pressed two fingers against her temple. "Oh my God. I didn't even think about that."

"Are you okay?" He encircled her wrist with his fingers. "Do you need to sit down for a minute?"

"I'd rather get out of here." She jerked her thumb at the mess on the bed. "We can leave that."

"Wait." He strode across the room, shoveled Marten's things back into the suitcase, zipped it up and placed it in the corner. "Let's go." When they got to the elevator, Joe looked over his shoulder. "Too bad we didn't notice that camera before you literally looked into its lens. We could've pretended we didn't see it and I could've waited for the person who planted it."

Hailey punched the elevator button three times. "Too late for that now?"

"They know we saw the camera. They lost their element of surprise—and so did we." When the elevator opened onto the lobby, Joe dropped the device into a trash can. "Hope they like looking at garbage."

TWENTY MINUTES LATER, Hailey let the Jag idle at a stoplight. She flexed her fingers on the steering wheel. "Joe, would you mind spending the night at my place tonight? I— This isn't a come-on or anything. It's just after what happened to Ayala and finding that camera… I don't want to be in that big house by myself—security system or not."

"Do you have an extra toothbrush?"

"Tons."

"Then I'm your man."

Oh, she was beginning to believe that.

"Great." She punched the accelerator and the car leaped forward—pretty accurately mimicking her heart.

On the way to Pacific Heights, Joe theorized about the hidden camera and what Marten's key unlocked, but all Hailey could hear was *I'm your man*.

If only Joe meant it the way she felt it. She could be confusing Joe's natural protectiveness for genuine tenderness, but the way he touched her went above and beyond. Then he'd catch himself and draw back— except for tonight.

For all she knew, they could get to her place and he'd take up his post across the street again…after brushing his teeth with one of her many toothbrushes.

She drove into the driveway and opened the garage door. She pulled into the three-car garage that housed her father's '66 Thunderbird and her stepmother's Range Rover.

Joe whistled. "Now, *that's* a car."

"You can take it for a spin if you like." Hailey cut the engine and pressed her lips together. Did that sound like she was trying to bribe him?

"That would be the type of car I'd like to take on Highway 1 down to Big Sur."

"You've taken that drive before?"

"Not in a classic T-Bird."

Hailey stepped from the car and waved toward the open garage door. "We have to go back outside and through the front door. There's no connection from the garage to the house."

"I'm disappointed. I would've expected a car elevator."

She snapped and pointed her finger at him. "I'll have my dad get right on that."

She entered the code on the side of the garage door frame and turned away.

Joe caught her arm. "Don't you stay to make sure nobody sneaks into the garage while the door is closing?"

"If someone did that, it would trigger the garage door to go up again."

"You—" he touched a finger to her nose "—need to be more careful and aware of your surroundings. You think you're safe just because you're in San Francisco instead of Syria?"

"I know I'm not safe here anymore." She waited until the garage door settled and spun around again. "And maybe if I'd been more alert in Syria, I would've suspected that the people who kidnapped us wouldn't have been willing to just let us go. We should've known they weren't done with us."

"If anyone should've been suspicious, it was Siddiqi. He's a guide in the area, for God's sake. He should've known the drill."

Hailey stopped on the bottom step and twirled around to face Joe, almost meeting him eye to eye. "Get off that idea. Naraj didn't set us up. In fact, maybe he's in danger, too. I should ask Agent Porter to request a check on him."

"That might not be a bad idea. Did you ask Ayala about him? If she'd seen him?" He joined her on the next step, and his clean, masculine scent invaded her senses.

She bobbed her head up and down. "As a matter of fact, I did. She hasn't seen him around."

"Put it on your list for Porter." He nudged her up the stairs.

She opened the door, stepped aside to let Joe through and then immediately armed the alarm system.

The peephole in the center of the door caught her eye, and she peered through it. "It's just a peephole."

"That's good news." Pinching his shoulder, he rolled it back. "I could use a beer, if you're offering."

"You and me both." She pointed to the kitchen. "You know the way. I'm going to call the hospital again to check on Ayala."

While Joe strolled into the kitchen, looking more at home than she felt here, Hailey placed a call to the hospital. She got a different nurse this time, but the word must've gotten around, because this one reported Ayala's progress without hesitation.

Hailey unzipped her boots and padded into the kitchen, where Joe had parked himself at the center island, sipping his beer.

"Ayala's doing fine, resting and will be able to check out tomorrow. I tried calling her cell, but it's dead or she turned it off."

Joe slid a beer toward her on the granite counter. "Did they confirm the poisoning?"

"The nurse was willing to tell me how Ayala was doing, but she didn't give me any details like that. We'll have to ask her tomorrow when we pick her up."

"You're bringing her back here?"

Was that disappointment in Joe's voice?

"Of course. I'm not sending her to a hotel after what she just went through."

"Yeah, yeah, of course not." Joe took a gulp of beer. "What *did* she just go through? What was all that about? Someone followed us to the restaurant? Knew we were going to be there? Slipped something into that martini?"

"I don't know." She tilted her head and wrapped her hair around one hand. "What are you saying?"

"Why was Ayala so quick to yell poison? Didn't she just get through telling us she couldn't hold her booze? I imagine a martini in San Francisco is a powerful thing."

"You saw her." Hailey ran a fingernail down the damp label on her bottle. "She was passed out on the bathroom floor. Did that look like a woman who'd imbibed two appletinis to you?"

Joe lifted his shoulders. "I don't understand how someone could've poisoned her at that restaurant."

"The same way someone replaced a peephole in a hotel door with a mini camera."

"But they knew Marten was staying at that hotel. Who knew we were going to that restaurant, and why hit Ayala only? Why not spike your wine or even my beer?"

"For someone who's spent the better part of two days telling me my life was in danger because of that kidnapping, you're doing an about-face."

"Not at all. Your life *is* in danger...and so is Ayala's. I'm just not sure how this all went down."

"Maybe we'll have a better idea after talking to Ayala tomorrow."

Hailey took a sip of her beer and rolled her shoulders back, loosening up a few muscles...and a few inhibitions. "So, do you still live in Boston when you're not deployed?"

He put his beer on the counter and caught a bead of moisture with his thumb on the outside of the bottle.

The pause lasted so long, Hailey had a chance to gulp down another mouthful of beer.

"I don't live in Boston anymore. I have a place in Colorado—fresh air and a view ringed by mountains."

Warming to the subject, Hailey asked, "Is your family still there? Your mother?"

"My mom will never leave South Boston, but at least we got her settled in a nicer place."

Hailey's heart skipped a beat. "We?"

"My siblings and I—my two brothers and one of my sisters."

"*One* of your sisters? How many do you have? How many in your family?"

"Five of us—I have two younger brothers and two younger sisters. My youngest sister is still living with Mom, and she…has issues."

"I'm sorry." She let the words hang in the air between them. She didn't want to overstep the boundaries here and have Joe clam up.

He lifted and dropped his shoulders. "Nothing to be sorry about—she chose drugs and alcohol, following in our father's unsteady footsteps."

"I know what that's like. My brother was the same— never met an altered state he didn't want to try."

"He cleaned himself up?"

"Who knows? He must've cut back being around my father, because my father wouldn't tolerate that behavior, but I find it hard to believe Win doesn't indulge when he parties with the beautiful people in Manhattan."

"Win?"

"Winslow Chandler Duvall."

Joe snorted. "I'm sure Win and Jenny are going to very different parties to get their drink on."

"Different parties, same outcome."

He clinked the neck of his bottle with hers. "You

seem to feel guilty about everything and everyone else—why not Win?"

"Why would I feel guilty about him? My brother has had every opportunity in the world and chose to squander those privileges." She put her elbows on the counter and cupped her chin in one hand. "Do you feel guilty about Jenny?"

"Oh, yeah, and not just her."

"Not the rest of your family? If they're all helping out your mom, it sounds like they're doing okay."

"They're doing great. One of my brothers is a software engineer, the other's in law school, and my sister is a buyer for a big department store."

As he listed the accomplishments of his siblings, Joe's face almost glowed.

"You did that for them, didn't you?"

"Me? Hell, no. They're successful because they worked hard and stayed out of trouble."

"And because they had a big brother setting an example for them. Keeping three out of four on the right path is something to be proud of. What happened to Jenny?"

Joe's jaw tightened, and his eyes took on a dangerous glitter. "Fell in with the wrong crowd. People determined to see her fail."

"Boyfriend?" Hailey swirled the liquid in her bottle and took another swig.

"My ex-wife."

Hailey choked and the beer fizzed up her nose. She covered her mouth with her hand. "What?"

"My ex, Deirdre."

"I—I didn't know—didn't realize you'd been married."

"It was a long time ago. We dated in high school, and then before my first deployment, she got pregnant, so we got married."

As Hailey's world tilted sideways, she blinked. "You have a child?"

"Deirdre miscarried—and I wasn't even there."

"I'm sorry." She stroked the back of his hand with her fingers.

"When I got home, she blamed me for not being there, but I heard from other people, including my sister, that she'd been drinking and partying."

"Oh." Hailey pressed a hand to her heart. "Is that what led to the divorce?"

"It didn't help. It also didn't help that she'd tricked me into the marriage by getting pregnant on purpose. Told me she was on the pill, but that was a lie."

Hailey rubbed the back of her hand across her nose. Despite Deirdre's misdeeds, Hailey couldn't help but have a little pity for her. Once you had Joe McVie, how could you ever let him go?

"Wait—so is that why she targeted your sister? To get back at you?"

"I think so, not that Jenny needed much encouragement." Joe finished off his beer and clicked the bottle onto the counter decisively. "I failed both of them."

"You can't seriously blame yourself for Jenny's behavior."

"I ended the marriage, and it led to a downward spiral for Deirdre."

"Who wouldn't end it? Her reckless actions probably caused the miscarriage, and it sounds like that spiral started before the marriage ended."

"You take vows, you should make it work. I could've given it a try. She would've changed."

"Ha!" Hailey tipped her head back and laughed at the ceiling. "That never happens. Ever."

"I had other reasons for ending that marriage."

"You mean besides being tricked into it, losing your baby and being stuck with a hard-partying wife?"

"I'd met someone else."

Hailey's world tilted again, and she narrowed her eyes. "You cheated?"

"No, I'd just met this woman. There was nothing between us—then—but she and Deirdre couldn't have been more different. Deirdre represented everything I wanted to escape…and Lisette represented everything I wanted to run toward."

"Sounds like you wanted to escape from Deirdre before you ever met Lisette, and you would've ended the marriage even if Lisette hadn't made an appearance." She traced her fingertip around the lip of the bottle. "What happened to Lisette?"

"We dated briefly and then she dumped me."

"Uh-huh." As if any woman would dump this man.

"What does that mean?" He cocked his head.

"My guess—" she held up her finger "—is that you

felt guilty about Deirdre and made a relationship with Lisette impossible."

"Wow." He shook his head and ran a hand through his hair. "Not only did you get me to spill my guts, you psychoanalyzed me in the process."

She grabbed both of their bottles with one hand, dumped her beer out in the sink and placed the bottles in the recycling bin. "I figured it was about time. You came in knowing so much about me and my family."

"Because it's common knowledge, or at least there for the mildly curious."

"Is that what you are? Mildly curious?"

He encircled her wrist with his fingers. "There's nothing mild about how I'm feeling right now."

Hailey swallowed, wishing she had the rest of that beer she'd just dumped down the drain.

He dropped her wrist and stepped back. "I'm sorry."

"Don't apologize." She pushed some hair from her overheated face. "I'm guessing all the personal questions I threw at you gave our conversation an intimate quality even though we're…strangers."

"Is that what you think we are? Strangers?"

"I—I mean we barely know each other. We've been chasing after phantoms and keys to nowhere, and when we finally have a minute to catch our breaths and the conversation turns personal, we slipped into an easy familiarity."

"That's a lot of words." Joe raised his eyes to the

ceiling and then focused on her like a laser, his blue gaze smoldering. "I like you, Hailey, a lot."

"I like you, too." She ran her tongue around the inside of her mouth. "And I appreciate…"

He sliced a hand through the air. "I don't want you to appreciate me or be grateful or want me to be your bodyguard or your driver or your security guy."

"Is that how you think I see you?" She plopped back down on the stool, because her knees were in danger of giving out.

"Not sure." He brushed his knuckles against the stubble on his chin. "When you're not thanking me, you're outfitting me so I can be presentable for your fund-raiser."

Hailey's jaw dropped. "You're kidding. I guess I've been successful at keeping you at arm's length, then, because I've been trying like hell to keep my hands and my dirty thoughts to myself."

A slow smile spread across Joe's face, the kind of smile that made her heart do jumping jacks.

"Dirty thoughts, huh? Like what?"

She reached across the counter and grabbed a handful of his shirt, pulling him toward her. When they were nose to nose and she could see the faint freckles on his forehead, she said, "These thoughts are better expressed across a pillow."

Joe's nostrils flared right before he plowed his fingers through her hair, drew her close and planted his lips against hers.

The edge of the counter dug into her ribs and her

toes cramped as she curled them against the tile floor, but she never wanted this kiss to end.

He broke it off way too soon and coughed. "You're strangling me."

She blinked. "Sorry." She loosened her hold on his shirt and flexed her fingers.

"Are you going to lead the way to that pillow?" He folded his arms, tucking his hands under his arms. "Or have you changed your mind?"

"Because that kiss you laid on me was supposed to deter me?"

"It wasn't meant to deter or persuade. It just…was. If you haven't noticed, I've been trying to keep you at arm's length, too. I'm not sure I'm capable of that anymore, unless you want me to. Then I'll try like hell just to keep you close."

"That's a lot of words." She moved around the corner of the counter and cupped his jaw with one hand. "Why are we pretending? Why are we fighting against what's been clear from the minute we met on Fisherman's Wharf?"

"Because you have baggage and I have baggage. Because we don't know if this is real or we're feeling it because we have a shared threat hanging over us."

"Right now—" her hand slipped from his face to his neck, where she wedged her fingers beneath his shirt and caressed his warm skin "—I don't care about any of that."

He clasped her hand and raised it to his lips. He

kissed each one of her knuckles. "Right now, there's just this single moment."

Lacing her fingers with his, she took a step back and pulled him along with her. "You've never been upstairs, have you?"

"I've never been invited."

"I'm inviting you now. I even have toothbrushes up there."

"Then it's a done deal."

Still holding Joe's hand, she walked upstairs with him trailing behind her. She didn't say another word, afraid of breaking this spell between them.

Her bedroom door stood open. She dropped his hand and crossed the room to the window. "You have to see the view."

He stood still at the entrance to the room, his solid frame outlined by the doorjamb. He whispered across the darkness, "I'm looking at the only view I wanna see right now."

His words sent a thrill through her body, which tingled in all the right places. She never would've guessed Joe McVie would have all the right moves *and* all the right words.

She stretched out her hands. "Come to me, Red."

His long stride ate up the distance between them, and he took her hands, squeezing them lightly.

She made room for him at the window, and their shoulders nestled together. Dropping her head to the side into the crook of his neck, she said, "Isn't it beautiful?"

He draped his arm over her shoulder and twisted his head to the side to look at her. "The most beautiful view I've ever— Oh my God, get down!"

And the tender moment ended with Joe hooking his arm around her neck and yanking her to the ground as glass shattered around them.

Chapter Ten

As his heart practically jumped out of his chest, Joe caught a bead of blood on Hailey's cheek with the pad of his thumb.

"Are you hit? Are you all right?"

"Hit?" Her glassy dark eyes widened. "Hit by what? Why did you throw me down? Where'd the glass come from?"

Joe ran his hands over her body in a poor imitation of what he'd had planned for her in that giant bed. "Hailey, the glass is from the window. Look."

She raised her eyes to the window that looked out on the spectacular view of the bay, which now sported a jagged hole. "What happened?"

"Someone took a shot at you through the window."

Her body, still safe beneath his, jerked. "What do you mean?"

"Someone had you pinned down with a laser on your forehead. Thank God I saw it before he got off the shot."

She began to shake. "No. That can't be. That's not possible. It was a light from the street."

"A red dot of light on your forehead?" He wrapped his arms around her trembling frame. "I'm Delta Force, remember? I know what a night-scope laser looks like."

She buried her face in his chest. "What if you hadn't come over to look at the view?"

"Not possible. You called and I came." He kissed the top of her head and then brushed some slivers of glass from her hair. "Can you move? I want you to crawl to the bed and then get on the other side of it, on the floor."

"Where's my phone? I'm calling 911."

"Your phone's downstairs. Use mine and do it behind that bed." He handed the phone to her, closing her fingers around it. Rolling from her body, he said, "Move."

"Where are you going?"

"Going to pop my head up and have a look."

She stopped midcrawl and grabbed his shirt. "No, you're not."

"Just a peek. Get on that phone."

She huffed out a breath but continued a damn good army crawl across the carpet.

Joe got on his knees in front of the window and yanked the drapes closed. He parted them at the middle and put his eye to the glass at the bottom of the window.

"What is that building across the street from you?"

"That's a house."

"It's huge. Who lives there?"

"Some stockbroker and his wife and kids. I don't think he'd be renting out any rooms to snipers."

"Are they home?"

"I don't know. Hang on."

As he listened to Hailey make the 911 call, he continued to scan the scene across the street. "There's that small park. There are several trees tall enough to give someone a view of this room."

"The police are on their way." She sucked in a noisy breath. "Joe?"

His heart stuttered again. "Are you okay?"

"I'm fine, but I think there's a bullet in my wall."

"Good. Let's leave it for the police to dig out."

"Someone shot at me through my window from a tree? Do you see anyone in the park?"

"Nope. Maybe he made his escape after he took the shot, while we were on the floor."

"Maybe he thinks he hit me."

Joe did another scan of the park and then crawled toward Hailey. He found her stretched out on the floor, on her back, clutching his phone to her chest.

She flung her arm out to the side and pointed to the wall. "Bullet."

"You're right. At least the police will be able to identify the type of weapon used."

"And the FBI. I'm reporting this to Porter, along with the attempt on Ayala's life. Someone is desperate to shut us up, whether we have anything to say or not."

"That's a bold move, all right."

Sirens screamed from the street below, and Hailey rolled her eyes. "That'll get the neighbors talking."

"Are you ready?" He touched the small cut on her cheek. "The glass hit you. Scared the hell out of me when I saw the blood."

"Better the glass than the bullet." She grabbed his hand and kissed the inside of his wrist. "Thank you for saving my life."

"Anytime." He nudged her to start crawling out of the bedroom. "You first."

She rolled onto her stomach. "I suppose we should stay down just in case he's waiting out there to take another shot through the window."

"At least until we get out of the bedroom." He scooted to the side to let her pass. "I'm actually glad the shooter took aim at you first."

"Thanks." She kicked her foot out at him as he crawled behind her.

"Think about it, Hailey. Would you have noticed a red dot on my forehead? If he'd taken me out first, you would've been in shock, confused and an easy mark for his next shot."

"You're right. I literally would not have known what hit you…and then me." She shifted to her side when they reached the hallway. "Okay to stand up now?"

"The police are at the door."

One of the officers pounded on the heavy door and shouted, "Police! Did someone call the police?"

Hailey scrambled to her feet. "I guess that's me."

ABOUT AN HOUR LATER, the police left and Hailey collapsed in a chair in the living room. "So, somebody climbed a tree in the little park across the street and took aim at my bedroom window."

"That's what the officers seem to think after finding that broken branch, but your neighbors didn't see or hear anything except your window shattering." He sat on the arm of her chair and brushed her hair back from her forehead. "You still have a few grains of glass in your hair."

"Don't cut yourself." She shook her head back and forth. "I hope Agent Porter follows up with the SFPD. He said he would when I talked to him tonight."

"Call the police department tomorrow to make sure they're going to send the report to Porter, like they said they would."

"I will." Hailey yawned and curled her legs beneath her. "Do you think they came after us once they saw us nosing around Marten's hotel room?"

"Maybe. It's clear they haven't found anything in his hotel room, either, but they must think whatever he had or was going to say is important enough to risk raising a red flag for you and Ayala, because you two weren't going to refute the story about Denver being among your kidnappers."

"We need to find out what the key opens." Hailey yawned again and her eyes drifted closed.

Joe swallowed his disappointment. This night hadn't ended the way he'd anticipated, but he couldn't expect

Hailey to be in the mood after a sniper had put her in his crosshairs.

He smoothed a fingertip over the small cut on her face. He'd thought at first his attraction to Hailey had come from his memories of Lisette, the woman who had been out of his league and out of his reach years ago, but Hailey and Lisette occupied two different planes.

Lisette frittered away her parents' wealth on selfish pursuits and status items meant to dazzle the poor boy from the wrong side of the tracks. Hailey put her father's money to good use, helping others. Hailey used wealth as a tool, a means to a very good end.

And in the process, her goodness had done more to dazzle this poor boy than all the gold in Fort Knox could.

"Hailey." He slipped an arm beneath her back. "Do you want me to carry you up to bed?"

She murmured and burrowed deeper into the chair.

He pushed up from the arm of the chair and grabbed a knitted blanket from the back of the couch. He shook it out and tucked it around her body. Then he kissed her cheek and whispered, "Good night, Hailey."

Holding his hands out, he backed away from her sleeping form. He dashed upstairs, found the promised toothbrush and brushed his teeth. Then he grabbed a blanket from the bed that had been reserved for Ayala. As he reached for the pillows, he stubbed his toe on a hard edge beneath the bed. He flipped up the bed-spread and nudged Ayala's laptop farther under the bed. He swung by Hailey's room and snatched a pillow from her bed for good measure.

When he got back downstairs, he wedged her pillow on the right side of Hailey's body and threw the other two at the couch.

He eyed the length of the couch and shrugged. He'd spent the night in worse conditions than a too-short couch in a Pacific Heights mansion with a beautiful woman sleeping in a chair across from him.

He toed off his shoes and pulled down his jeans and socks all at the same time. He unbuttoned his shirt, yanked his T-shirt over his head and folded everything into a neat pile on the coffee table.

He settled one half of the blanket on the couch, anchored it with his body and pulled the other half on top of him for a cover. It took him several minutes to get comfortable. He made the best of it by rolling to his side and hanging one leg off the edge of the couch.

On his side, he had a clear view of Hailey snuggled into the chair. He had no intention of leaving her downstairs on her own.

What worried him was the growing feeling that he could never leave her side again.

HAILEY TURNED HER head and caught her breath. Was the crick in her neck from sleeping in a chair all night or from Joe's life-saving technique of tackling her to the ground?

She rubbed her eyes, and a vision appeared before

her. She rubbed her eyes again to make sure she wasn't dreaming, and the vision only got clearer.

Joe's bare leg hung from the couch, his toes touching the floor, the blanket slipping off his muscled thigh. The other edge of the blanket draped across his torso like a toga, and he certainly did resemble a Greek god.

The muscles she'd imagined and felt beneath layers of clothing appeared before her in an awesome display of maleness.

If that shooter had to take aim at her last night, why couldn't he have waited until after she and Joe had made love? How inconsiderate of him to ruin the moment.

"Is the chair that comfortable?"

Hailey jerked upright. Joe's words wrenched her gaze from his perfect pecs to his slightly amused blue eyes. She pulled the afghan close around her body as if she were the one half-naked and exposed.

"This chair is extremely comfortable. I've crashed here on more than one occasion, usually with a book or tablet abandoned on my chest."

"I felt bad about leaving you in the chair. I thought about carrying you upstairs to bed when you fell asleep, but I didn't want to wake you and I didn't want you sleeping in that drafty room with the shattered window."

"That's fine, but you didn't have to take the couch. I told you there were plenty of rooms upstairs." She punched the pillow under her head. "Hell, you could've taken my room if you don't mind a nice, brisk temperature."

"I didn't want to leave you…here by yourself."

His low voice rolled over her like a warm breeze.

She tucked her hands beneath her cheek. "I'm sorry we were interrupted last night."

"I'm sorry someone took a shot at you."

"And were you also sorry we were interrupted?"

"What do you think?"

"I—I think you don't want to appear callous by being more upset our carnal desires weren't satisfied than the fact that someone tried to kill me."

He grinned and her heart melted around the edges.

"That's a fine line to walk. Can we agree that we're pissed off at that sniper for trying to kill you *and* for splashing cold water on our…carnal desires?"

She pulled the afghan up to her nose and peered at him over the edge. "I can agree to that. Can we also agree that the danger is gone and maybe it's time to return to our original plan?"

He threw off his blanket and placed both feet on the wood floor. "Danger? What danger?"

Hailey squirmed beneath her cover. The only danger she could see now was the fire in Joe's blue eyes.

Before she had a chance to answer his rhetorical question, Joe tossed the blanket behind him and crossed the space between them on his knees. He pulled the lever to recline her chair and she shot forward, her feet swinging to the floor.

He crouched before her and said, "I didn't undress

you last night when you fell asleep because I didn't want to...take liberties."

Gripping the arms of the chair with both hands, Hailey lifted her hips. "By all means, take as many liberties with me as you like."

Joe unbuttoned her jeans and tucked his thumbs beneath the waistband on either side. He yanked down her underwear along with her pants and pulled them from her legs. He threw them over his shoulder, never breaking eye contact with her.

A thrill skipped through her body, anticipation making her mouth dry. She didn't have to wait long.

Joe hooked his arms beneath her knees and pulled her forward. He positioned her legs over his shoulders and tucked his hands beneath her bottom.

When his lips touched her throbbing flesh, the world stopped spinning for a split second. When it started again, it seemed to careen out of control. She dug her fingernails into his scalp as if that could ground her.

His tongue toyed with her, teased her, and she panted out his name. He stopped his exquisite torture, but she craved more.

She gasped. "You can't stop now."

"I thought that's why you were saying my name... You'd had enough."

"You're a tease." She yanked on his earlobe. "Why are you even talking?"

"Yes, ma'am."

He buried his face between her legs and resumed

his exploration of her body and all its sensitivities—and he was a fast study.

Her hands slipped from his russet hair to his shoulders, which she squeezed and molded as he kept taking her to unimaginable heights of pleasure.

She reached the precipice of her climax a few times only to have Joe shift his attention to her inner thigh or to a freckle just above her mound. Her frustration quickly morphed into a searing need that built up in her core and heated her blood beyond the boiling point.

After yet another detour, Joe swept his tongue across the pulse beating between her thighs. The ache in her belly exploded into a million pieces, and she arched her back, driving herself against Joe's mouth.

He didn't pull away, which made her orgasm tumble into infinity, wave after wave of pleasure engulfing her body.

Drained and sated, she slumped back against the chair, her legs still dangling over Joe's shoulders.

He eased back, cupped her heel and kissed the arch of her foot. "How was that?"

She opened one eye. "You have to ask? That was incredible."

"Hard to deliver something to the woman who has everything."

"I do now." She wiggled her toes at him. "Well, almost everything."

"What else can I give you?"

"For starters, you can slip off those boxers and let me do what I do best."

"What you do best?" He raised one eyebrow.

She placed one foot against his chest. "You said it yourself. I'm the giving type, generous to a fault."

"I don't remember saying it was a fault of yours." He hooked his thumbs under the waistband of his boxers and pulled them down his powerful thighs.

Her heart rate, which had been returning to normal, spiked again. She slid from the chair and knelt in front of him, wrapping her arms around his waist.

"You know what?" He scooped his hand into her hair. "I didn't even properly kiss you."

"Whatever you just did couldn't be called 'proper,' so I'm not holding my breath for a proper kiss, either."

He hunched forward, pulling her head toward him and slanting his mouth over hers. His tongue, which had just teased her to crazy heights of pleasure, continued its assault as his lips pressed against hers.

When he finally released her, breathless and wanting more, she gasped. "If that's a proper kiss, sign me up for propriety."

Joe rose to his feet and started to take his place in the chair, but she wrapped her hands around his calves.

"I want to taste you, too." She took his erection into her mouth and skimmed her tongue along the length of him.

He moved against her and sucked in a breath. "I can't last long like this." He gasped. "Especially when you do *that*."

He pulled away from her and sat in the chair, yanking her down on his lap. "Is this a very expensive chair?"

She straddled him. "Very."

"Oh, well."

He plunged into her and she rode him. At one point the chair flipped back into a reclining position, but it barely put a hitch in their rhythm—and they did have a rhythm.

Having Joe inside her felt more right than anything she'd ever experienced. He seemed attuned to every nuance of her body to bring her maximum pleasure, which made her feel safe in his arms.

When her climax took her this time, it flooded her body, rocking her gently up and down. That blissful ease didn't last long as Joe reached his own pinnacle. He thrust against her madly, hungrily, clawing at her backside in a futile effort to purchase some stability.

It didn't work. He yelled and howled like a crazy man and took them both over the side of the chair.

They lay on their sides, their limbs entwined, laughing and gasping, clinging to each other as if they'd never let go.

Hailey didn't want to ever let go.

When the pounding on the front door started, reality came crashing down on their pretty dream.

Chapter Eleven

"Ms. Duvall? It's Agent Porter."

Joe groaned and flung his forearm across his eyes. "I can't believe the FBI is interrupting my postcoital haze."

"Is that what this is?" Hailey scrambled to her feet and lunged for her jeans and panties.

She still had her top on, and Joe couldn't believe he hadn't explored those beautiful breasts along with the rest of her body.

As she stepped into her jeans, she nudged his bare backside with her toe. "Move. I'm not inviting Porter in with you sprawled out on my floor naked."

"I would hope not." Joe gathered up his clothing, the pillows and both blankets and headed up the stairs, two at a time.

He slipped into Hailey's bedroom, chilly from the cold air seeping through the hole in the window. Porter's banging on the door and this cold slap to the face both served as reminders of his true mission here in San Francisco—and that wasn't to finally land the rich girl.

The murmur of voices carried upstairs. He tossed Hailey's pillow back on her bed, messed up the covers and dropped the knitted blanket on the foot of the bed. Then he dragged the other blanket to the guest room Ayala was supposed to occupy before she was poisoned at dinner and put it and the pillows back on the bed.

He clicked the door closed, made up the bed and got dressed just as Hailey led Porter upstairs.

He pressed his ear to the guest room door and heard Hailey's voice. "I had a friend with me and he noticed a red dot on my forehead and pushed me down."

"Where's your...friend now?"

"He went home. You don't need to talk to him, do you? He doesn't know anything, and the cops already interviewed him last night."

"The police took the bullet?"

"Dug it right out of the wall over here."

The voices faded out to the point where Joe could just hear a word or two.

He paced the room while he waited, feeling ridiculous hiding out. Would Porter even know who he was? Recognize his name? He didn't want to take any chances. Major Denver needed him active and engaged, not sidelined and reprimanded. So, for now he'd hide out like a thief in the night.

He walked past the bed for the hundredth time and

kicked the cord connecting Ayala's laptop to an outlet under the bed.

Finally, he heard the front door slam and Hailey's footsteps on the stairs.

She tapped on the door. "Are you decent?"

He called back, "Does it matter?"

The door swung open, and Hailey stood on the threshold, one hand on her hip. "I was hoping you weren't."

He swooped toward her and kissed her mouth, just because he could. "How'd it go? Did you finally get Porter's attention?"

"Oh, yeah." She wrapped her hands around his waist and tucked her hands in his back pockets—probably because she could. "He figures it was a high-powered rifle, and this time, unlike the car on the sidewalk, whoever took aim at me had deadly intent."

"No kidding. You told him about Ayala?"

"I did, and he's taking that seriously, too. I also asked him to check on Naraj and if he'd heard anything from the UK about Andrew yet."

"And?"

"The FBI was actually one step ahead of me. They've tried contacting Naraj, but nobody can find him." She bit her lip and shook her head at him. "Don't even say it."

"What about Andrew Reese?"

"MI6 hasn't contacted him yet, or at least the CIA hasn't let Porter know anything about Andrew. I think Porter turned over the request to the CIA, so they're looking into Andrew's whereabouts."

"Gotta love that cooperation between agencies. Do you see now why my teammates and I are taking the investigation of Denver into our own hands? We can't get anyone to believe us about the conspiracy, even after what Cam and Asher uncovered."

"I think I'm making some progress with Agent Porter, though. That sniper attack on me rattled him... and he's not easily rattled."

"The Fibbies tend to be a stoic bunch." Joe ran a hand through his hair. "I need a shower if we're going to head over to the hospital and pick up Ayala."

"She won't be discharged until later today, but let's get breakfast and I have a few last-minute errands to run for the event." Placing her hands against his chest, she whispered, "I'd offer to shower with you, but then we'd never get out of here."

"God, I'm glad you're safe." He enfolded her in his arms.

"Thanks to you. I'm glad you accosted me on Fisherman's Wharf. I don't know where I'd be if you hadn't."

"Maybe you would've been safer." He rested his chin on the top of her head. "Maybe they're targeting you because of me. If you'd kept your head down, accepted that Marten had changed his mind about the meeting and had gone about your business as usual, you might not have ended up with a red laser beam on your forehead."

She stepped back from him, and strands of her hair stuck to his chin, keeping them connected. "Don't be dumb. Marten involved me the minute he contacted me when he got here, the minute he decided to leave me a key."

"You might be right."

"I am right." She placed her hands on his shoulders and squeezed. "And if you hadn't been around to protect me, I'd be in big trouble right now…or dead."

A knot twisted in his gut, and he pulled her close again, inhaling the musky scent of morning sex that clung to her body. His own body responded, and he took a step back so she couldn't feel his erection. He cleared his throat. "When are you getting that window fixed?"

Her gaze dropped to his crotch as a smile tugged at one corner of her mouth. "I'll call someone today to fix that… The window, I mean."

"You have a dirty mind, Ms. Duvall." He pinched her chin between his thumb and the side of his forefinger.

"You have no idea, Captain McVie." She patted his backside before spinning around. "But unless you plan to use what you're packing there, we need to get ready to go to the hospital."

"Towels?"

As she reached the bedroom door, she looked over her shoulder. "That was a fast recovery. Should I be insulted?"

"Even the thought of a cold shower will do that to a guy, so no."

"Clean towels and everything else you'll need are in the bathroom."

She swept out of the room, and he said to the closed door, "Not everything I need."

LATER AS HE sat beside Hailey in the Jag, he turned toward her. "Do you think Ayala will be able to make it to the fund-raiser?"

"If she doesn't have any lasting effects from the poison, she should be okay, but I don't know if she'll want to attend now. Why would she want to broaden that target on her back, especially once she hears what happened last night?"

"She didn't seem that enthusiastic in the first place."

"Yeah, she's shy and definitely doesn't like to brag about her efforts."

"I got that. Didn't seem interested in talking about the refugee center at all. Most of the time, people who do work that's close to their hearts like that can't stop talking about it."

"Ayala's reserved." She swung into the passenger loading area on the side of the large hospital's emergency entrance. "I think we can leave the car here as long as we're picking up a patient."

"And if we can't, you can always drop your father's name."

She threw the car into Park and pointed a finger at him. "I'm gonna take that as a joke, McVie."

"I'm only half joking. I'm getting accustomed to the perks afforded by Ray Duvall."

She snorted and exited the car.

The parking attendant tucked a ticket beneath the windshield wiper of the Jag, and Joe took Hailey's arm as they walked into the cavernous hospital.

They passed the emergency waiting room, and a man called out to Hailey.

Joe's protective instincts flared, but before he could embarrass himself again by taking down one of Hailey's friends, Hailey waved to the man.

"Patrick, how's it going?"

"Great." Patrick walked toward them, a slight limp hindering his gait. He gave Hailey a hug, and a different kind of instinct flared in Joe's gut.

Hailey pulled away first and gestured toward Joe. "Patrick, this is my friend Joe. Joe, Patrick."

As he shook Patrick's hand, Joe childishly applied more pressure than necessary. What made it worse was that Patrick's eyes twinkled, reading him like a cheap paperback novel.

Hailey touched Patrick's arm. "I hope you're not here for yourself."

"Naw—" he jerked a thumb over his shoulder "—one of the guys took a fall this morning."

Joe gazed over Patrick's shoulder at a transient, holding his head in his hands.

Hailey followed Joe's line of sight. "Patrick runs a homeless shelter in the Mission District."

"Mission Hope." Patrick jingled a large key chain in his hand. "Hailey's foundation has contributed a lot of money to our cause."

As usual, Hailey brushed off the praise. "Tax deduction."

Patrick's keys fell out of his hands, and Joe stooped to retrieve them. "Let me."

He scooped up the keys. As he shook them out, his pulse jumped. "What is this key?"

"Which one?" Patrick's eyebrows created a V over his nose.

Joe plucked out a key with a round cardboard tag attached to it. He studied the tag, but the writing on it in pencil had been smeared off—just like another key.

"That's a key to one of the lockers at the shelter."

"The shelter called Mission Hope. *M-I-S-S...*"

Hailey's eyes widened as she snatched the key from Joe's hand. "It looks the same. Marten knew about my work with Mission Hope, knew I'd been there before."

Patrick's head turned from side to side as if he were watching a tennis match. "What are you two talking about and can I please have my keys back?"

"Sorry." Hailey dropped the key chain into Patrick's outstretched palm. "Someone left me a key, and we've been trying to figure out what it unlocked."

"Do you have it on you?"

Hailey patted her pockets. "I left it at home, but it looks the same, doesn't it?"

"It sure does. Patrick, what did the writing on this circle say before it was wiped off?"

"'Mission Hope.'"

Joe asked, "Who gets keys to those lockers?"

"They're first come, first served. If a homeless person comes to the shelter and has valuables, or at least what he considers valuables, he can leave them in a locker while he's sleeping at the shelter or when he goes out to panhandle." Patrick extended his hand to Joe. "You're welcome to come by and check out the lockers at any time…as long as you bring a check or some food or toiletries. Nice to meet you. I have to get back to Michael."

Joe shook the man's hand—without the extra pressure this time. "Thanks. We'll do that."

"Great to see you again, Patrick." Hailey gave him a hug.

Patrick returned to Michael and sat next to him in the plastic chair.

Seemed he was surrounded by do-gooders. Joe touched Hailey's back. "Looks like we found the match to our key."

"I think so. Marten was at the shelter for some reason and thought it was a good idea to get a locker."

"Maybe because he figured nobody would think to look in a locker at a homeless shelter—except for his philanthropic friend who just might recognize a key from Mission Hope."

"As soon as we get Ayala settled at my place, we'll grab that key and pay a visit to Mission Hope with food and toiletries in hand."

Hailey checked in at the desk and joined Joe at the wide double doors leading to the treatment rooms of the emergency wing.

"The nurses told me she's doing fine and is ready to leave."

They found Ayala's bed, which occupied one of four curtained-off areas in a large room.

Hailey whipped back the curtain and rushed to Ayala's bedside. "Oh my God. How are you doing? I was so worried when I found you on that bathroom floor."

Ayala, her dark head propped up against a snowy-white pillow, gave Hailey a weak smile. "I can imagine."

Hailey whispered, "Was it poison? Did the police come by and talk to you?"

Ayala gave a shake of her head. "It wasn't poison, Hailey."

"What?"

Joe pushed a chair against the backs of Hailey's legs before she collapsed, and she sank into it.

He put a hand on Hailey's shoulder. "What did the doctors say, Ayala?"

She shrugged, and the hospital gown slipped from one shoulder. "A stomach upset and too much alcohol."

Hailey hunched forward. "You don't believe that, do you?"

"I don't know what to believe. I've been drunk before. This didn't feel like too much alcohol. Maybe it was all our talk before, but I immediately thought someone had poisoned me."

"But the doctors didn't find any poison in your

system." Joe sucked in one side of his cheek. "I suppose there are certain poisons that can be masked."

"Are there?" Ayala folded her arms. "I wouldn't know, but I do want to get out of here."

Hailey squeezed her hand. "We're here to pick you up and take you back to my place, but I should warn you, someone took a shot at me through my bedroom window last night."

Ayala gasped and clutched the sheet. "This is crazy. You should get out of this city, Hailey. We both should."

"I'm planning on it, but not before the fund-raiser. You'll be safe at my place for now. How are you feeling?"

"A little weak, but fine. They did pump my stomach, so if it was some kind of stealth poison, it's out now." Ayala closed her eyes. "Hailey."

"Yes?" Hailey shot a sidelong glance at Joe.

"I can't do that gala now. I'm sorry. I just want to get back to Florida."

"Of course. Don't even think about it."

A nurse bustled into the area, clutching paperwork to her chest. "Ms. Khan, you just need to sign a few forms and you're on your way." Ayala scribbled her signature a couple of times, and the nurse left some papers with her. "Hope you're feeling better."

Ayala swung her legs off the bed. "I'll feel better when I get out of this hospital gown and away from the guy hacking up his guts next to me."

Hailey stood up and retrieved Ayala's neatly folded

clothes from a shelf. "Will you be okay if we leave you at my place on your own for a while?"

"Sure. Why?" Ayala took the bundle of clothing from Hailey.

Joe gritted his back teeth. Why did Hailey feel the need to spill the beans to everyone? That key was need to know, and Ayala Khan didn't need to know.

"We think we might've found out what Marten's key unlocks."

"Oh?"

"By chance, I ran into a friend of mine who runs Mission Hope in the Mission District, and he had a key on him that looks just like Marten's."

"Be careful, Hailey. I still think you should let this go. I'm not sure the doc knows what he's talking about. That was poison coursing through my veins." She held out one hand to Joe. "Tell her, Joe."

"You know Hailey better than I do."

Ayala sighed. "You're right. Just take care of her. Now, if you two don't mind, I'm going to get out of this ugly gown."

"We'll be in the waiting room." Hailey patted Ayala's hand. "Take it easy."

Joe kept quiet down the corridor, which buzzed with new arrivals, a crying baby and nurses weaving in and out of the rooms. When they got back to the waiting room, he plopped down in a plastic chair that wobbled beneath him.

"That was strange."

"Ayala? I know. Why was she so sure it was poison?"

"Maybe she lied to get out of the speech at the fund-raiser."

Hailey punched his thigh as she sat down. "Be serious. It could've been poison that the doctor didn't or couldn't detect."

"That's a possibility." Joe nibbled on a rough cuticle on the side of his thumb.

"Are you biting your nails over this?" Hailey grabbed his wrist and folded both of her hands around his.

"Don't tell me you're going to send me in for a manicure before the big event." He splayed his free hand in front of him. "Delta Force don't do manicures."

"I prefer your rugged hands to a pair of soft, polished ones."

"Good."

"Whatever got Ayala, it spooked her."

"Shh." Joe tipped his head toward the double doors as the subject of their conversation walked into the waiting room.

Hailey tilted her head at him. "I don't know why you want to keep her in the dark about everything."

"I don't know why, either. Habit." But the words fell on deaf ears as Hailey launched herself toward her friend.

Joe stayed put, rising from his chair when the women approached. He pasted on a concerned expression. "All ready?"

"So ready to get out of here." Ayala hooked her hand through Hailey's arm. "It totally slipped my mind, but an Agent Porter from the FBI visited me right before you showed up."

Hailey whipped her head around. "He did? I met with him this morning about the shooting and told him about you. That was fast. What did he say? He didn't tell you about the shooting?"

"He didn't mention it, and he didn't have much to say about anything else once he saw my toxicology report. There was nothing in my system except alcohol."

Joe allowed the women to exit before him, and Hailey pulled out her car keys and punched the remote. The Jag beeped once.

Joe opened the door for Ayala, and as she slid into the back seat, he asked, "If you saw Porter before, didn't he tell you about the sniper shooting at Hailey?"

"Oddly enough, he did not." She dipped her head to reach for her seat belt, and her long hair hung like a curtain over the side of her face.

"Did he tell you why he was visiting you and how he knew you were at the hospital?"

Ayala snapped the seat belt in place. "He said Hailey told him about my incident last night."

Joe shut the back passenger door and climbed into the front. "Agent Porter never mentioned the shooting to Ayala. Isn't that odd?"

"You said it yourself." Hailey cranked on the engine. "Fibbies play it close to the vest."

"Did I say that?"

"Or maybe you were talking about Delta Force."

Hailey peeled out of the parking lot. "Are you hungry, Ayala?"

"Ugh, the thought of food literally turns my stomach right now. I'll take some tea when we get back to your place, though…and I'll get it myself. You two should head over to Mission Hope. Maybe you can put a stop to all this once you check out that locker."

"We can only hope."

When they arrived at the house, Hailey pulled the car into the driveway. She turned to Joe. "You can wait here. I'll see Ayala in, show her around the kitchen and head right back down."

Joe clicked open his door. "I need the exercise."

Hailey caught her breath, realizing he still wanted to keep tabs on her. "Sure you do."

Joe kept Hailey and Ayala in front of him as they climbed the stairs. As always, he'd kept watch to make sure they hadn't been followed, even though the bad guys knew exactly where Hailey lived, and now he had to look out for snipers in the treetops.

Safely inside, Hailey patted the couch that had served as Joe's bed last night. "Have a seat. I'll make you some tea."

"Don't be silly. I can walk into the kitchen and make a cup of tea."

"Let me at least get it ready for you." Hailey charged into the kitchen as if she were ready to turn out a full-course meal instead of boiling some water.

Joe took up a station near the front window. "Should we check that security footage, Hailey?"

"We can do it when we get back. Do you want some water or anything before we head out again?"

"Just a glass of water, please."

Hailey held a glass to the ice maker on the outside of the fridge and filled it with water. She took a few steps out of the kitchen when the teakettle blew.

Ayala pushed up from the couch and sauntered into the kitchen, taking the glass from Hailey. She brought it to Joe and joined him at the window. "See anything interesting out there?"

"Thanks." He took the glass from her. "Not much. Not high enough to see the bay, either."

Hailey called from the kitchen, "Milk?"

"Yes, please." Ayala rolled her eyes at Joe. "Really, I can make my own tea."

Hailey ignored her and continued banging around the kitchen. "What are you going to do the rest of the afternoon? You should take a nap. Bed's all ready for you."

"Maybe."

Joe took a gulp of water. "And your laptop is still under the bed."

Ayala jerked her head around so fast, Joe thought she saw something out the window.

"Did you see something?"

"I—I thought maybe something by the bench in that little park." As she pointed out the window, the red stone on her ring caught the light, flashing a beam on her face not unlike the one centered on Hailey's forehead last night.

Joe cupped his hand over his eyes as he peered through the window. "I don't see anything. Hailey's house has an alarm system. Just stay away from the windows and you should be safe enough here."

"Tea time." Hailey carried a steaming mug into the living room. "I left a few more tea bags on the counter for you, the kettle's on the stove and milk is in the fridge if you want more."

"Thank you so much. I'll be fine here—go."

Hailey swept Marten's key from the counter and grabbed her purse. As she hoisted her bag over her shoulder, she turned at the door. "Set the alarm when you get the chance—5806."

Ayala waved.

When they stepped onto the porch and Hailey had shut and locked the dead bolt, Joe poked her in the side. "Now you have to change that code as soon as you get home."

"I had to give it to her. How else was she going to arm it?"

"Just sayin'. Reset it."

Hailey saluted. "Aye, aye, Captain."

"I'm not in the navy." He poked her again. "Are we taking your car?"

"There's parking around the back, and I know Patrick's car, so I can block him in if I have to."

"There you go with your friends in high places again."

As they got in the car, Joe glanced up at the window, partially obscured by the bushes in the front garden. The drapes stirred and then dropped into place. "Looks like Ayala didn't waste any time setting the alarm."

Hailey said, "Good. She seemed nervous."

"She thought she saw something in the park." Joe clicked his seat belt.

"Did she?"

"It was her imagination. There was nothing there."

Hailey nodded. "Yeah, nervous."

Hailey navigated like a pro through the busy San Francisco streets, driving past Union Square, where the Christmas tree still towered above shoppers.

Two blocks later the shoppers had thinned out, replaced by shopping carts pushed by raggedy men and women looking to score a quick buck or two.

"How often do you come down here?"

"Not enough. My assistant, Gretchen, delivers care packages from the foundation occasionally." She hit the steering wheel. "Shoot. We forgot to bring the food and toiletries."

"I'll write a check instead. I'm sure there are a fair number of vets out on the streets here. Let me feel the glow of a good deed for a change."

"I have a feeling you do plenty of good deeds." She wheeled around the back of a gray stucco building sporting a neon sign announcing the Mission Hope, only the *P* and the *E* had burned out at the end.

Joe nudged her and pointed at the sign. "I'm sure that's not what Patrick wants to advertise."

Hailey giggled. "It could be worse if the *I, O* and *N* on the end of *mission* were also burned out."

She parked behind a black Prius with a Coexist bumper sticker.

"Let me guess." Joe leveled a finger at the car. "That's Patrick's."

"That's why I'm parking here."

Joe kept a tight hold on Hailey's arm with one hand and a tight hold on the barrel of his gun with the other as they walked through an alley leading to the back door of the shelter.

A few homeless guys loitering with cigarettes dangling from their lips held out their hands. Joe brushed past them.

When they stepped inside, a cook hovering over a boiling pot called a welcome without looking up. "Dinner doesn't start for another few hours and you can't start lining up for another hour—around the front."

"Actually, we're here to see Patrick."

The cook glanced up from his work. "Oh, sorry. Yeah, Patrick's out in the van rounding up some poor souls for dinner."

"That's okay. Are the lockers still in the front room, on the other side of the dining hall?"

"They are." He put his spoon down and swiped a

towel across his forehead. "You lookin' for something in particular?"

Hailey held up the key and dangled it in the light. "Just checking on my friend's locker."

"Okay, go ahead, then. What was your name again?"

"It's Hailey. Hailey Duvall."

"Ah, why didn't you say so? I know the name, and now I know the beautiful face behind all that generous giving."

"This place couldn't run without people like you." She closed her hand around the key and backed out of the kitchen.

She led the way past a dining area with rows of empty picnic tables lined up. "The locker room is on the other side of this."

A couple of transients looked up from their card game as Hailey and Joe walked by a common room.

Hailey entered another room where banks of metal lockers hugged the walls. Some of the lockers had keys hanging from them.

Joe flicked one of the familiar keys with his finger. "How much to rent one?"

"I think it's still a quarter." She placed her hands on her hips and surveyed the room. "There's no number on this key chain, so I have no idea which one it belongs to."

"I'm wondering how these guys remember which lockers are theirs, especially if they come in here drunk or drugged out."

"They're not allowed in here when they're high."

"Let's face it. Some of them are just high on life, if you know what I mean—they're in a permanently altered state without any substances to help them along."

"I'm sure Patrick and the rest of the staff help them out."

"We don't have that luxury right now." He banged his fist on the first locker to the right. "You ready to try your luck?"

"At least we can rule out the ones that already have keys." She stepped forward and tried to insert Marten's key in the first locked locker. "Nope."

Hailey tried the lockers on the top row, with no results, and crouched down to start on the bottom row.

A transient with a hat pulled halfway over his face shuffled into the room, and Joe nodded at him.

The transient tipped his head and then stuffed his hands into the pockets of his bulky overcoat, mumbling to himself.

"None of these." Hailey popped up, bumping Joe's arm with the top of her head, noticing the homeless guy in the corner for the first time. She zeroed in on him and said, "Do you need help finding something?"

Joe tapped the side of her boot with his toe.

She scowled at him, reserving her smile for the transient. "Can we help you?"

"No!"

Hailey jumped back at the shout and put a hand to her throat. "All righty then."

"Keep moving, Hailey." Joe tapped the next locked locker.

She inserted the key, and it clicked. "This is it."

Out of the corner of his eye, Joe detected a flash of movement. He reached for his gun, but the fake homeless guy beat him to the punch.

By the time Joe spun around with his weapon in hand, the transient had his arm around Hailey's neck and a gun to her head.

Chapter Twelve

Hailey twisted her head to the side and tried to sink her teeth into the arm that held her, but the man tightened his grip and she choked.

Joe stood in front of them, blocking Marten's locker, his gun pointed at the man who held her.

The man, who didn't smell homeless at all, shoved the cold metal of his gun against her temple. "Don't even think about it, or I drop her right here. Place your gun on the floor and kick it toward me."

"Don't do it, Joe. He's going to kill me anyway. You know what happened at the house."

Joe waved his gun at the man. "Who are you, and what do you want?"

The man chuckled, his hot breath blasting her ear. "I'm holding all the cards here. Why would I tell you anything? Now step aside so I can get whatever it is de Becker left there for Hailey."

Hailey blinked rapidly at Joe and mouthed the word *move*.

Without releasing his gun, Joe took a few shuffling steps to his right.

The man spit out, "More."

Hailey gave Joe a wink, and he moved farther from the locker but still kept his gun trained on Hailey's captor.

The man descended on the open locker, dragging Hailey with him and keeping one eye on Joe.

He probably didn't want to shoot her here because of the men in the other room playing cards. A gunshot in a homeless shelter would be a very big deal. Of course, once he took her out of here, all bets were off...if he did take her out of here.

Still facing Joe, the man made a half turn toward the locker and plunged his hand inside the small space, the sound of his fingernails scrabbling across the metal echoing in the room. "What the hell?"

He made another sweep of the empty locker and ended it with a thump of his fist. "What did you do with it?"

"There was nothing in there."

"Liar." He pushed Hailey back, and her head banged against the bank of lockers.

Joe growled and took a step forward.

"Don't move. I swear I'll kill her."

"You're not going to shoot anyone in here. This place probably has a hotline to the SFPD."

Joe's cold voice had her swallowing hard. How could he be so sure?

"Look, I don't have anything. I didn't take anything

out of that locker because it was empty." She spread her arms out to the sides. "Search me."

Someone laughed from the other room, and the man's eye twitched.

What would he do if they were interrupted? Would he start shooting? She couldn't allow that to happen.

"Take me out of here, and I'll show you. I have nothing on me."

"Hailey, no." Joe moved closer. "I'm not going to let him take you anywhere."

"What the hell is going on in here?" Two of the men from the card game stumbled into the locker room and hovered at the doorway, their eyes wide as they looked from Joe's gun to her captor's.

"None of your business. Get the hell out of here… losers."

The two men turned, and then one of them grunted and charged at Hailey and the man holding her.

The attack surprised her captor. He swung his gun from Hailey's head toward his oncoming attacker and took a shot.

Hailey screamed.

Joe lunged forward and pushed her behind him.

The homeless hero fell on top of the shooter and they grappled on the cement floor, the gun between them.

Joe raised his own weapon, taking aim at the two men rolling on the floor.

"Be careful, Joe. Don't hit the homeless guy."

Cheers and shouts filled the room and Hailey's

mouth dropped open as she saw the men crowding the doorway and rooting on their guy as if this were an MMA fight instead of a life-or-death struggle.

Joe got closer to the melee on the floor and shouted, "Stop. Stop."

A shot sounded, and Hailey covered her ears as the sound bounded off the walls. She plastered herself against the lockers, her mouth dry as she watched the two men on the floor slowly separate.

The transient rolled off the other man, breathing hard and clutching his bloody leg. He coughed and then laughed like a crazy person.

Hailey's gaze shifted to the man who'd had her at gunpoint.

Joe crouched beside the form sprawled out on the cement, blood pumping and spurting from a wound on his chest. Joe had his fingers at the man's pulse and was furiously whispering something in his ear.

Patrick stormed into the room. "What the hell happened here? Someone call 911. Trace, are you okay?"

The transient on the floor groaned and rolled to his side. "The guy shot me in the leg. They saw it. Self-defense, man. He had a gun on that woman."

Patrick stepped away from the carnage on the floor and grabbed Hailey's arm. "Is this true?"

"It's all true. That guy—" she pointed at the man expiring on the floor, Joe still beside him "—had a gun on me, and Trace came in here and charged him."

Joe straightened up, rubbing his hands on the thighs

of his jeans. "He could've gotten Hailey killed, and himself, but Trace definitely saved the day."

Trace grabbed his bloody leg. "The guy called us 'losers.' I'm no loser. I'm a US marine."

An hour later, Hailey slumped behind the wheel of the Jag with Joe beside her. "Since you're all over that police report, is it going to get back to your superiors?"

"Oh, yeah. I'm just glad Trace kept his mouth shut about *my* gun. That would've been a whole lot harder to explain without a concealed-carry license here in California."

"I'm just glad the guy didn't decide to shoot me first before Trace got to him."

"Trace had the element of surprise going for him. Never been happier to see a marine." He traced a finger down her throat. "It's still red. The only thing I regret is not killing the bastard myself."

"You were too busy worrying about me." She smoothed a thumb against the crease between his eyebrows. "Did you get anything out of the dead guy?"

"What do you mean?"

"I saw you talking to him, or at least trying to talk to him as he lay dying. Did he give you any answers to your questions?"

"He was too busy trying to catch his last breaths." He patted his jacket pocket. "I did get his prints, though—just in case the SFPD doesn't care to share his identity."

"I stuck as closely to the truth as possible—my friend left me a key to his locker at Mission Hope and that man attacked us and held me at gunpoint to get whatever was in the locker."

Joe massaged his temples. "Which was empty, anyway."

"Not. Quite." Hailey slid a slip of paper from inside her bra and proffered it to Joe between thumb and forefinger.

He jerked forward. "You got this out of the locker?"

"My hand was already inside the locker when the fake transient made his move. I snatched the piece of paper and shoved it down my top, pretending to hold my hand against my heart."

"I'll be damned." He punched on the dome light with his knuckle and read aloud. "'I'm still alive. MDB.'"

"Marten. Marten's still alive."

"And this—" Joe waved the slip of paper in the air "—is how he decided to tell you? That son of a..."

Hailey snatched the paper from his hands, crumpled it up and swallowed it.

His eyebrows jumped to his hairline. "Why'd you do that?"

"I don't want anyone to see it. Nobody needs to know that Marten survived that push or fall or jump from the ferry." She patted her stomach. "Nobody knows."

"I think you're taking this subterfuge a little overboard." He smacked the dashboard. "He put you in all kinds of danger by leaving you that key just to tell you he was among the living."

"I don't think that was his original intent, Joe. I believe he left me something in that locker, and when he survived, he returned to the shelter to collect it and replaced it with that note."

"You're probably right. That makes the most sense." He drummed his fingers on his knee. "Why hasn't he come forward with his info yet? It would be stupid to change his mind now because the people after him don't care and wouldn't trust him, anyway."

"He must be in hiding, waiting for the right moment."

"The right moment is now, to protect you and get these people off your back. Doesn't he realize he's put your life in danger with his silly spy games?"

"Maybe he's not aware of the attempts on my life."

Joe clenched his jaw. "He should've been able to figure that out. He knew people were following him. He knew enough to arrange a secret meeting with you and to leave you the evidence in case something happened to him."

"I'm just amazed Marten was able to survive in the bay that night."

"You heard Joost. Marten was some kind of Olympic swimmer."

"That survival is a story I hope to hear someday—straight from Marten's lips." Hailey started the engine and cranked up the heater. "I hope Trace is going to be okay. What do you think the police are going to find out about the dead guy?"

"Probably whatever his bosses want them to know.

That's why I took his fingerprints myself." Joe sawed his lower lip with his teeth as he stared at the alley behind the shelter.

"What's wrong?"

"The twenty-five-million-dollar question."

"Which is?"

"How the hell did anyone know about that key? How did that man know we would be at the shelter at precisely that minute?"

"He followed us from the house."

"Dressed as a transient?"

"He…he— Wait." She braced her hands against the steering wheel. "You can't be implying that Patrick had anything to do with this."

"Patrick? He's not the only other person besides us who knew about the key and the shelter."

Hailey knitted her brows. "Not Ayala."

"She's the only person outside of Patrick and us and maybe Joost who knew about the key."

"That's not possible." A flash of heat claimed her body, and Hailey turned down the car heater. "Ayala was attacked last night. Poisoned."

"Was she? That's not what the toxicology report indicated."

"But we all agreed that the poison could've been something undetectable. She passed out in the bathroom. I saw her, felt her clammy skin."

"That could've been the result of anything—even playacting."

Hailey clutched her hair at the nape of her neck

as her head swam. "Are you saying you think she set up the whole poisoning scene? For what possible purpose?"

"For this purpose." Joe drew a circle in the air with his finger. "To throw us off her trail. If Ayala is a victim just like you, how could she be responsible for the attacks on you?"

"Joe, this is crazy. I worked with Ayala for over a year in the refugee center."

"What did you learn about her in that time? You said she was reserved. Where's her brother? Her husband?"

"Husband? She doesn't have a husband."

"Fiancé? She wears a ring with a single red stone on the ring finger of her left hand."

"She does?"

"She was the only one of you, Marten and Andrew who didn't ID Denver. Just like the poisoning, she's trying to keep a low profile. Here I was thinking Siddiqi was the mole when it could very well be Ayala. She knows the area, the language, the people."

"That's just it. She cares for those people. You haven't seen her in action."

"She might care for them on one level, but they'll never trump her ideology. I've run across several extremists. They don't think like the rest of us do."

Hailey pinned her unsteady hands between her knees. "You think she came out here to monitor the situation? Gain my trust and then strike?"

"I do. Maybe her associates had already put the

plan with Marten in motion, and when they realized Marten had communicated with you, they sent for her to cozy up to you, find out what you knew or suspected."

"You were suspicious of her from the beginning, weren't you? Maybe it was your instinct kicking in when you first saw her that told you she posed a threat to me."

"I took her down because I thought her umbrella was a gun."

"Makes perfect sense to me, because an umbrella looks just like a gun." Tipping her head back, she closed her eyes. "I still can't believe it. You might be wrong."

"I'm not wrong, Hailey. Nobody else could've tipped off the gunman that we were at Mission Hope looking for Marten's locker."

"So she got on her phone as soon as we left the house and alerted someone."

"She did it before that—when we left her to get dressed in the hospital. She knew about the key then. Who knows? She could've even left something in this car, like a GPS to track us. She could be on her computer right now cooking up the next plot."

"She didn't bring her laptop."

"Yes, she did…" Joe snapped his fingers. "Now I know it's her. She told us she didn't have her computer, didn't she?"

"That's why she didn't see my email. She doesn't

like reading emails on her phone and said she didn't have her laptop."

"She does have it. She left it charging under the bed, and I stubbed my toe on it while I was waiting for you to finish up with Porter this morning."

"Oh my God. So she lied about the computer. What else?"

"A lot." He turned toward her and grabbed her arm. "Hailey."

"What?" His tone sent a river of chills down her spine.

"She knows I'm on to her."

"How do you know that?"

"I mentioned that she could pass the time this afternoon on her laptop, totally forgetting she wasn't supposed to have it here. It gave her a start when I said it."

Hailey shook her head, trying to clear the fuzz in her brain. "When we show up alive, she's going to be even surer that we're on to her."

"If she hasn't heard from her contact by now, she's going to assume the plan didn't work. She already knows we're on to her."

"And she's alone in my house."

"I doubt she's going to be hanging around, but step on it anyway."

Hailey squealed out of the lot behind the shelter and made good time, despite the traffic. She hoped Ayala wasn't there. She wouldn't know what to say to her. How did you confront someone you thought was your friend but who was capable of such evil?

As she pulled into the driveway, Joe put a hand on her arm. "Let's take it easy."

"You said she wouldn't be here." She clenched the steering wheel, her white knuckles practically glowing in the dark. "I don't want to see her...ever again."

"I do. I want to finish what I started when I first laid eyes on her, but she's not gonna be sitting in that chair with a cup of tea waiting for us."

"Then what are we waiting for?" Hailey yanked on the door handle.

"Hailey, we don't know what kind of surprise she might've left us. Her henchman at the shelter wasn't successful, and these people don't give up."

Hailey ducked her head. "Don't tell me there's going to be another sniper waiting for me in the tree across the street."

"I don't know what might be waiting for us. That's why we're going to be careful and take it slow and easy." He swung open his door. "Wait for me."

In the rearview mirror, Hailey watched Joe shrug out of his jacket. When he reached the driver's-side door, she cracked it open for him.

"Okay, come on out, slowly."

She grabbed her purse from the center console and hugged it to her chest as she slid out of the car.

Joe stepped around her immediately, placed his body between her and the sidewalk, and draped his jacket over her head. With one arm firmly around her shoulders, he walked her up the steps.

She stumbled once or twice, but Joe steadied her.

"No red laser beams on the back of my head?"

"Nope. We're almost at the door. Keys."

As she handed him her key chain, she tossed off the jacket and looked over her shoulder. "Safe here?"

"Yeah." He stretched up and felt along the top of the doorjamb, his fingers trailing over the wood. Then he knelt down and inspected the base of the door and curled up one corner of the mat.

Hailey held her breath through the search when a thought hit her square in the chest. "The food. She could've even poisoned my food."

"Good point." Joe slid the key into the lock and turned it slowly. He released a breath when it clicked. "Get behind me when I open the door, Hailey."

She licked her lips. "Do you think she set up an automatic firing squad when the door opens?"

"I wouldn't put anything past her. Would you?"

"Now that I know she's responsible for the carnage at the refugee camp? No." She took a sideways step to huddle behind Joe's solid frame, putting one hand on his back.

He eased open the door, every muscle in his back tensed and ready for...something.

"No firing squad." Still feeling exposed on the porch, Hailey started forward, her purse swinging from her hand.

Joe shouted, "Hailey, stop!"

A funny smell assaulted her nostrils, but before she had time to analyze it, Joe grabbed her around the waist and pushed her over the back of the porch into the garden below.

And then the world exploded around her.

Chapter Thirteen

The ringing in his ears drowned out Hailey's screaming, or maybe no sound was actually coming from her mouth, wide-open and showing off all her pearly whites.

Joe rolled onto his back, the branches of some bush gouging his bare skin. Black smoke billowed from the porch, the acrid wisps swirling around him, causing his eyes to water.

Voices came from somewhere. He shook his head and spit what looked like dissolved charcoal out of his mouth.

Hailey. His head fell to the side and some leaves scratched his face, but he got a good look at Hailey next to him—in one piece. Maybe.

"Are you hurt?"

She choked in response, and black spittle formed at the corners of her mouth.

The voices he'd heard before seemed to be closer now, and with great effort, he turned his head away from Hailey.

A clutch of people had gathered on the steps up to the house and were leaning over the railing into the garden where he and Hailey had landed like a dazed Adam and Eve.

Joe moved an arm and then a leg. They still seemed attached to his body. The fall into the various bushes and plants had done more damage to him than the bomb had.

Because that was a bomb—not a very good bomb, but it probably could've torn them to pieces if they, instead of Hailey's purse, had crossed that threshold.

Joe struggled to extricate himself from the thorns and sticks that clung to his clothing and skin, trying to make him part of the mulch.

He didn't want to be mulch. He snatched his arm away from a particularly vicious bush and scooped it beneath Hailey's back, lifting her up. "Are you all right? Say something to me."

Her dark eyes clicked into focus, and then they widened and she let loose with a scream right in his face.

It was the sweetest sound he'd heard in a long time. "Are you hurt? Let me help you up."

One of the neighbors on the steps yelled out, "We called 911. The fire department is on the way, but it looks like the sprinkler system shut down the fire. Is Hailey okay?"

Joe finally maneuvered into a crouched position just as one of the onlookers decided to clamber across the front garden. Since the garden sloped down to the street, the man lost his footing and started to slide down.

Joe held up his hand. "It's okay. I've got my bearings now. I'll help Hailey. She doesn't seem to be hurt, but she's still in shock."

The sirens racing toward the scene were the second sweetest sound he'd heard today.

Joe gently pulled Hailey toward him with one hand while detaching her from her thorny bed with the other, as she whimpered.

He whispered as he worked. "You're fine. You're gonna be okay, my love."

The sirens stopped, and a commotion erupted on the street as the firefighters unraveled their hoses.

Just as Joe had Hailey up in a seated position, a firefighter clomped into the garden with his boots and protective gear.

Joe called out, "Careful. There's an incline. We're being held in place by a few strategically placed bushes."

"Were you thrown by the explosion?"

"We jumped."

"Probably a smart move."

Another firefighter joined him with a stretcher on his back. "Let's roll her onto this. Does she have any other injuries?"

"Not that I can tell, but she's still in shock. She gets clarity every now and then and screams bloody murder, but her most serious injuries are from the fall and this damn foliage poking us."

They secured the stretcher next to Hailey and eased her onto it.

"You need a stretcher?"

"No, but I'm coming with her in the ambulance and don't even try to stop me." Joe stood up and hoisted one end of the stretcher.

When they got free of the garden, Joe tipped back his head and surveyed the damage to the door. The explosives had blown the door off its hinges, and it now lay on the sidewalk at the curb. It must've sailed over him and Hailey, and he said a silent thanks to God that it hadn't landed on them.

They loaded Hailey into the back of the ambulance, and Joe climbed in after. On the ride to the hospital, the EMT checked her vitals, cleaned her superficial wounds and put an oxygen mask on her face. Through it all, Hailey maintained consciousness but couldn't seem to speak or make sense of what was going on around her.

Joe kept hold of her hand, stroking the back of it with his thumb and murmuring ridiculous sentiments like how he'd never leave her side and he'd take care of her forever.

He cranked his head around to the EMT. "Where are you taking her?"

"San Francisco General, emergency."

"You're not taking her to the emergency room. She's going to a private room and seeing a doctor who isn't too busy to spend more than thirty seconds with her."

The EMT opened his mouth, and Joe sliced his hand through the air to silence him. "Do you know who this is? This is Hailey Duvall. Her father, Ray Duvall, practically owns San Fran Gen. So just do it."

The EMT hunched forward and stuck his head into the cab of the ambulance.

Joe glanced down at Hailey. Was that a smile playing about her mouth underneath that oxygen mask?

He leaned down and touched his lips to her ear. "I learned from the best, baby."

An hour later, with Hailey tucked into a hospital bed in a private room with an IV in her arm, Joe pulled up a chair and laced his fingers through hers.

"Feeling better?"

She croaked in her new raspy voice, "I'm fine. What about you? Has anyone checked you out yet?"

Lifting up his shirt, he twisted around to show off the bandage on his back. "That's the worst of it. Some sharp branch speared me. Why didn't your father's gardeners plant some ice plant in that area?"

"Let's be thankful there weren't more rosebushes in there."

"There were enough." Joe held out his arm where a hodgepodge of gauze patches created a pattern on his skin.

She kissed her fingertips and pressed them against the biggest gauze square. "Did the police talk to you yet?"

"They did, and Agent Porter is on his way." He

scooted his chair closer to the bed. "Turns out Ayala must've gotten a C in bomb-making class."

"I don't know." Hailey folded over the edge of the sheet and creased it with her fingers. "That sounded like an A-plus effort to me."

"She didn't use enough chemicals to take down the house, but we definitely would've been severely injured if we'd stepped across that threshold."

"My purse set it off, didn't it?"

"I saw the wire inside the house at about the same time you moved forward and swung your purse in the doorway."

"You saved us again. If you hadn't seen the wire, hadn't suspected Ayala of setting us up, the EMTs would've been picking up our body parts from that front garden." She covered her eyes with one hand. "It felt like…felt like…"

"What you experienced at the refugee camp." Joe smoothed his hand over her leg beneath the sheet.

"Only that was much worse. There was shrapnel with that one, horrible, horrible injuries. How could a nurse perpetuate that kind of violence?"

"Something else is more important to her now. If a few children have to die for the greater good, she's down with that."

"Exactly." Agent Porter tapped on the open door. "We're looking into Ayala Khan's brother and her boyfriend."

"Agent Porter, this is Joe McVie."

Porter stepped into the room, his large frame making it appear even smaller, and extended his hand to Joe. "I know all about Captain McVie, Delta Force. You've been busy on your leave, Captain."

"Call me Joe. I feel like we're old friends."

Porter drew up a chair on the other side of Hailey's bed. "Are you okay, Hailey? You've been through the wringer since…Joe showed up, haven't you?"

"You think I'm a target because of Joe?" She struggled to sit up, punching a pillow behind her. "If you're going to blame anyone, outside of the real culprits, blame Marten de Becker…and help him. He's still alive."

"So is Andrew Reese."

"Thank God. Is he talking?"

"I got nothing from the CIA except Reese took a beating and refused to finger his assailants."

"Unlike me."

Crossing his arms, Joe extended his legs beneath Hailey's bed. "What are you doing about Ayala Khan?"

"We have her on the terrorist watch list, the no-fly, and we've contacted Interpol. Everything we can do."

"Is the CIA ready to admit Major Denver didn't have anything to do with the bomb in Syria?"

"Hold on." Porter held out a hand. "All we know is some group is targeting the relief workers who were kidnapped. We don't know why. Maybe they think they can ID their captors."

Joe snorted. "I don't think some random terrorists

in Syria would be too worried about that. The connection is the ID of Major Denver and the fact that Marten de Becker, who had positively identified Denver as one of the kidnappers, decided to change his mind."

"You're making a lot of assumptions, McVie."

"Are you forgetting what my Delta Force teammates discovered? The original emails implicating Denver were fake, and the claim that Denver shot an Army Ranger when he went AWOL was force-fed to Asher Knight through mind control." Joe bunched his hands into fists and shoved them into his pockets.

"I heard some of that."

"Those claims that Major Denver kidnapped the aid workers and planted the bomb for their car to take back to the refugee center are also false. This is one big setup."

"I'm not here to get into that with you, McVie. I'm here to make sure Hailey is okay—" Porter flashed his teeth at Hailey "—and to glean any more information she might have about Ayala Khan."

"It sounds like you already know more about her than I do." Hailey took a sip from her water cup beside the bed. "I didn't know about any boyfriend, and I had no idea her brother had links to any terrorist organizations."

Joe hunched forward, elbows on knees, and asked, "Do you know anything about a boyfriend or fiancé?"

"Nothing yet. How do you know she has one?" Porter's eyebrows collided over his nose.

"How *do* you know that?" Hailey grabbed a napkin to dab at the water she'd spilled on the front of her hospital gown.

"I'm just guessing, because she wears a ring on her left ring finger." Joe shrugged. "A lot of times women get lured into these causes with some misplaced sense of romanticism."

"We'll be looking into any and all of her contacts."

Joe felt Hailey's gaze boring into him and glanced up to meet her narrowed eyes. "I—I'm just generalizing. Most women have minds of their own."

Porter rescued him by asking Hailey another question and then stayed on another twenty minutes, taking notes about what Hailey remembered of Ayala's day-to-day activities at the camp. Then he tucked his notebook into his breast pocket and pushed up from the chair. "I'm glad neither one of you was seriously injured. You were lucky to have Delta Force on your side when you went back to your house, Hailey."

"I've been lucky to have Joe around on several occasions." She flicked at the IV running into her arm. "Agent Porter, can Marten come to you with his information?"

"Any of you can come to me at any time. I thought I made that clear in the first set of interviews stateside." He squinted at her. "Why? Have you had contact with de Becker?"

"Not yet, but I'm sure it's coming. He's alive and he wants to stay that way. The only insurance he has is the truth. Once that's out, there's not going to be any more reason to silence him."

Porter lifted his linebacker shoulders. "There's always payback."

Hailey's face drained of color, and Joe jumped from his chair. Pumping Porter's hand, he said, "Thanks for coming by."

As Porter reached the door, Hailey called out, "I expect to see you at the fund-raiser tomorrow night, Agent Porter."

The Fibbie spun around at the door and smacked the wall. "You're still going through with that?"

"Of course. I wasn't injured in that blast, and it's great advertising for what we're battling out there."

"If you plan to be there, the SFPD is going to have to ramp up security."

"I'm counting on it." She winked at him.

When he left, Hailey sank against her pillows again and closed her eyes.

Joe perched on the edge of her bed and traced a line from her temple to her jaw. "Are you sure you're up for the gala?"

"Oh, yeah." Her dark lashes fluttered on her cheekbones. "I have a feeling about tomorrow night."

"I have feelings about tomorrow night, too, and none of them good."

"That's why we have to carry on with our plans. Dark forces are surging in this city, and they're going to converge at the Pacific Rim tomorrow night. My fortune cookie said so."

"Whoa, that's deep." He pinched her soft earlobe. "Hailey?"

Her breathing had the deep, rhythmic quality of someone in REM, which didn't surprise him, as some of that juice in her IV was a strong sedative to help her cope with the shock of the explosion.

Joe straightened out her covers, tucking them beneath her chin. He kissed her parted lips and then returned to his sentry position beside her bed.

As he slumped in the chair, stuffing a pillow behind his back, he said, "My fortune cookie told me to take a chance on a dark-haired beauty—and am I glad I did."

A BRIGHT LIGHT FLASHED. Black smoke curled in the distance. A horrible stench like hellfire permeated the air. And the children screamed. The children screamed.

Hailey shouted and kicked out her limbs.

The side of the bed dipped, and a warm hand clasped hers. A soft touch smoothed the hair back from her forehead.

Her eyelids flew open, and a savior with red hair hovered above her.

"Shh. You're okay. You're in the hospital and I'm right here with you."

And he'd never leave her. Didn't he say that before? He'd never leave her side again.

She threw her arms around Joe's neck. "Oh, God. The dreams. The visions."

"The explosion at your father's house brought it all back, every wretched detail." He stroked her glossy hair. "You should see someone, Hailey, a professional."

"You're probably right." She tried to swallow, but with her parched throat, it ended in a cough.

"Here you go." He handed her the water cup and placed the straw in her mouth. "You seemed to be sleeping soundly before. Do you want the nurse to give you some more sedative?"

"Oh, God, no." She slurped up every last drop of the water. "That stuff makes me thirsty, and I think it's partially responsible for giving me hallucinations. What time is it, anyway?"

"It's five a.m. The gala is tonight, if you're still game."

"Damn straight." She eyed Joe's tousled hair and scruffy chin. "You've spent another night in less-than-ideal conditions, haven't you? Let's see—since we've met, you've spent one night in a park across the street from my house, one night on a too-small couch and now a night cramped in a chair. You need a good night's sleep in a real bed."

"I intend to spend a night in a real bed, real soon, but I can do without the sleep." He quirked his eyebrows up and down at her.

So, he didn't intend to rush off the minute the danger ended?

"That can definitely be arranged. Now, when can I get out of here?"

"Whenever you like. You're a VIP, remember? But

let's not take off just yet. There's a small problem. You can't stay at the Pacific Heights house."

"Oh, boy." She smacked the heel of her hand against her forehead. "I need to call my father."

"He already knows."

"What?"

"He's already called the hospital once." Joe slipped his phone out of his pocket and dropped it on Hailey's lap. "Do you want to call him? It's eight o'clock in New York."

"Might as well get this over with." She entered her father's number in Joe's phone. "He's not going to answer an unknown number." To his voice mail, she said, "Dad, it's Hailey. Everything you heard is true. I'm in the hospital after an explosion at the house. Call me back at this number."

She ended the call, keeping the phone cupped in her hand. "In five, four, three, two…" Joe's phone vibrated. "Dad, it's Hailey."

"What the hell is going on out there? Why is someone rigging a bomb at the Pacific Heights house?"

"I'm fine, Dad." She winked at Joe.

"Don't play that pity card with me. I already know you're fine. I talked to Dr. Owens for a good twenty minutes. He told me you were in perfect health except for a few bumps and scratches. What he couldn't tell me is why someone is bombing my house."

"It has to do with—"

"Don't tell me. It's that Syria mess, isn't it? Give it up, Hailey. You've put your life in danger too many times to count. Come back to the fold and get back into the business. Your brother's a pretty face, but he's useless on the day to day. I need you."

"I don't like the way you do business, remember? And if you haven't changed your ways, I wouldn't think you'd want me around to blow the whistle on your unethical practices again." This time she avoided Joe's gaze, which she felt burning the side of her face.

Her father harrumphed over the phone. "You think I give a damn about that now? You ratted us out, I paid my fine and it's over. I'd still rather have a snitch like you around than Win."

"A snitch?"

"Face it, that's what you are, Hailey. A snitch and a do-gooder."

"Someone else I know calls me a do-gooder."

"Smart man."

"How do you know it's a man?" Hailey met Joe's questioning blue eyes with a smile.

"You think I'm a fool? You think I don't know you? Dr. Owens also informed me that you have some military guy keeping watch over you there like some kind of damn bodyguard. If you're letting some man that close to you, it means something."

"It does, Dad."

"Good. Then get that door repaired once the cops let you back in and keep this military guy close."

"Oh, I will." She ended the call and pressed the phone against her heart.

Joe propped on the frame of her bed. "You blew the whistle on your dad's company?"

"One of them. He was engaging in unfair business practices, bordering on the criminal."

"Sounds like he still wants you back."

"I guess things aren't working out with Win, but what he wants first is for me to repair his house." She handed the phone back to Joe. "I didn't even see it. How bad was the damage? I know there was a fire."

"Your father's extensive sprinkler system put that out quickly. Like I said, Ayala flunked bomb making. The door landed on the sidewalk, the foyer is scorched, and you and I pretty much destroyed that front garden."

Hailey snapped her fingers. "All fixable."

"But not livable. You won't be able to stay there until the police and the FBI finish their investigation. You're welcome to stay with me at my hotel in Fisherman's Wharf. I'll even buy you another chowder bread bowl."

"Better yet, you're welcome to stay with me at *my* hotel."

"Your hotel?"

"The Pacific Rim."

"You mean that place where the forces of evil are converging?"

"That's the one."

"I'd be honored."

AFTER SHE WAS discharged from the hospital, Hailey

used Joe's cell phone to place a few calls while a car took them to Joe's hotel to pick up his things.

When they finished at Joe's hotel, Hailey braced herself to face her father's house and the damage there. What she faced was yellow police tape ringing the property and a patrol car stationed out front.

The officer got out of his car when she and Joe stepped onto the sidewalk. "Can I help you?"

"I'm Hailey Duvall." She waved her hand at the house behind her. "This is my father's house, and I'm just here to pack a bag and take a look at the damage."

"Just be careful on the porch. The investigators are almost done."

"Will do." She kicked Joe's suitcase on the side-walk. "Put these in the garage by the Jag. We'll take the car over to the Pacific Rim."

Joe wheeled his bag into the garage and parked it at the rear of the Jag. "Ready?"

On shaky legs, Hailey climbed the steps. Joe must've sensed her trepidation, as he kept a firm hand at her back.

He pointed into the foliage to the right. "That's where we landed."

"Looks painful."

"It was." He picked up a chunk of cement on the top step. "Part of the porch."

"Nice of them to return the door." Hailey nodded at the scorched and splintered door leaning to the right of the gaping entrance to the house.

Black burn marks smudged the doorjamb and the

porch. Evidence of water damage from the sprinkler system and the fire hoses stained the wood floor in the foyer, and a scorched tapestry decorated the wall.

"I hope that wasn't expensive."

"It's all expensive, but my father has insurance." Hailey sniffed the air and swallowed. Smell more than anything triggered her memories. She covered her nose and mouth.

"You doing okay?" Joe rubbed a circle on her back.

"Yeah. Let's get this over with. Can you take some pictures of the damage? I'm going to send them to my dad, and he can forward everything to his insurance company."

While Joe took out his phone, Hailey glanced around the living room to make sure Ayala hadn't helped herself to some valuables on her way out.

She caught her breath when she saw the mug with Ayala's lipstick on the rim. She hadn't even processed Ayala's betrayal yet—her betrayal of the people who'd counted on her in the refugee camp, yes. That was stunning. But the personal betrayal from a woman she'd admired and worked beside hadn't hit home yet. Hailey curled her hands around the sink and leaned forward. Just one in a long line of betrayals from people she trusted.

But not Joe. This whole journey with him hadn't just been about his dedication to justice for Major Denver, had it? Her involvement had definitely drawn the perpetrators out of the woodwork. If they hadn't come after her, Joe never would've been able to get close to Marten—at least not in the same way—and in her bed, in her heart.

She jumped as he touched her shoulder.

"Do you want to wait in the car? Just give me a list and I can pack up for you."

Swinging around, she threw herself into his arms. "You would do that, wouldn't you? For me. Just for me."

His arms, strong, secure, wrapped around her body. "Don't ever doubt me, Hailey. I would do anything for you. I'd go to hell and back to protect you, and even though you're completely out of my league…"

She put two fingers over his lips. "Don't ever say that again. Money is just money, Joe. It doesn't buy integrity, loyalty, courage. Hell, it doesn't even buy class."

"You have all of that *and* money." He kissed the corner of her mouth.

"If you think I have all those qualities, then I must be in your league and you're in mine." She returned his kiss, and as his hand cupped the back of her head, she never felt safer.

In an instant, those feelings of security evaporated as Joe's body jerked and he whipped out his weapon.

"Hold it right there. Don't come any closer."

Hailey twisted her head over her shoulder, her mouth dropping open at the sight of a raggedly dressed man waving a crutch in front of him.

"You don't wanna shoot me, man. I just came here to get that hat." He pointed to Marten's black hat on the coffee table. "And return it to its owner."

Chapter Fourteen

"Hey, you!" The patrol officer from the front of the house charged through the front door, his gun drawn. "Drop that crutch."

"If I drop the crutch, man, I won't be able to stand." The transient tapped his leg. "I got shot yesterday, saving this young lady's life...and that tough-as-nails D-Boy's, too, come to think of it."

Hailey blew out a breath and dabbled her fingers down Joe's corded forearm. "It's Trace from Mission Hope."

"You shouldn't sneak up on people like that unless you have a death wish...man." Joe pocketed his gun. "It's all right, Officer. We know this guy."

The young cop wiped a bead of sweat from his brow. "Ms. Duvall?"

"It's okay. Everything he said is true. I was... attacked yesterday and Trace saved the day. You can leave us."

The officer holstered his gun and squared his shoulders. "Don't do that again. When an officer tells you to stop, you stop."

"Yes, sir, Officer, sir." Trace saluted and pushed back his hood.

Hailey waited until the police officer walked through the gaping hole that used to be the front door and then took a few steps toward Trace with Joe hovering behind her. "Is your leg okay?"

"Just a flesh wound." Trace grinned. "I've had worse."

Joe cleared his throat. "You're straight with the police over the shooting? They're not filing any charges against you, are they? If so, we'll be happy to speak on your behalf."

Hailey nudged Joe with her elbow. "You're catching on. You could be Deputy Do-Gooder."

"Yeah, yeah. I'm good with the cops." Trace held up his middle and index fingers together. "Like this now. I didn't even shoot the guy. His finger was on the trigger, so he shot himself. I just directed the gun away from me."

"What brings you here?" Joe folded his arms over his chest, widening his stance. "How do you even know where Hailey lives?"

Trace leveled a stubby finger at the hat. "Told ya. I'm here to pick up something for a friend. He told me about the house."

"Where is Marten? He's alive?" Hailey dived for the black hat and skimmed her fingers across the rim.

"Isn't that what the note said?" Trace leaned on his crutch and fetched a cigarette from his other pocket.

Joe lunged for Trace and snatched the cigarette from his hand. "No lighting up in here. Are you crazy?"

"Some say I am." Trace tapped his head. "But you know about that kinda crazy, don't you, soldier?"

"Are you getting any help for that?" Joe handed the cigarette back to Trace. "Not in the house."

"Here and there. Couple of shrinks volunteer at Mission Hope." He pocketed the cigarette.

"How do you know about that note? About Marten?" Hailey twirled Marten's hat around her hand.

"Crazy dude, that Marten. Talks kinda funny, too."

Joe asked, "Where'd you meet him?"

"Met him on the rocks down by Fisherman's Wharf. He was comin' out of the bay like one of those escaped prisoners from Alcatraz."

Hailey shook her head. "No prisoners ever escaped from Alcatraz—and lived to tell about it."

"They never found that bunch, just their makeshift rafts." Trace winked. "You never know."

"Back to Marten." Joe tapped the toe of his boot.

"Yeah, came out of the water, told me he was hiding from some people and just faked his own death. I told him the best way to be invisible in this city was to be homeless. Got him suited up and took him to the shelter with me for a meal."

"Did he say he was pushed from the ferry?" Hailey perched on the arm of a chair. "Do you want to sit down?"

"Not staying that long." Trace scratched his scruffy beard. "Dude said he jumped."

"I thought he was dead."

"I guess that's what he wanted."

Joe glanced at her, his eyebrows peaked over his nose. "Nice of him to worry his friend. Is that when he got the locker, when he went to the shelter with you?"

"Yep. Saw the locker and figured it suited him just fine."

"Wait a minute." Joe held up his hands. "If he got that locker after he nose-dived off the ferry, how did he get that key to Joost?"

"Joost must've been lying."

"Joost is the big blond guy—" Trace held his hand a few inches about his head "—talks funny like Marten?"

"That's him." Hailey clenched her teeth.

"Then Joost lied, 'cause Marten dropped off the locker key with him after making a copy for himself. Then I guess Marten lived longer than he expected, because he went back to the locker and replaced the letter he had in there with the note telling you he was alive."

"How in the world did Marten expect me to know what that key unlocked?"

"Has 'Mission Hope' written right on it." Trace cocked his head.

"It was worn off." Joe rubbed the back of his neck. "Did Marten tell you to keep an eye on the lockers?"

"Yeah, and I did. I saw you two going in there and

I would've been there sooner if I'd noticed that guy following you, but I kinda got caught up in the card game. I still saved you, didn't I?"

"You did." Hailey flipped up the hat and put it on her own head. "Where is Marten now and what does he have planned next?"

"I don't know where he is. What he has planned next?" He tipped his head toward Hailey. "He wants his hat back."

Joe pushed off the sofa where he'd been leaning and jumped at Trace, causing him to drop his crutch. "You tell that selfish SOB to come forward now and admit the truth so Hailey doesn't have to keep looking over her shoulder. You see all this? It's all because of that crazy…dude, Marten."

Trace hopped backward, away from Joe. "I'll tell him, I'll tell him. Just don't follow me, man. Don't expect me to take you to him. He'll disappear again. He warned me about you."

"Joe." Hailey rose from the arm of the couch and rubbed his back. "Let Marten do it his way."

"While he plays games and puts your life in danger? Why should I?"

"Because he might just disappear, like Trace said, and then we'll have nothing."

Joe wagged his finger in Trace's face. "Tell him to hurry up or he's going to have another enemy after him."

"On it. I'm on it." Trace's gaze dropped to his crutch on the floor.

Hailey dipped down and retrieved it, tucking it beneath his arm. Then she swept the hat from her head and handed it to Trace. "Anything else? Would you like to take some food with you?"

"I could use a beer."

"Out." Joe pointed at the doorway.

Trace grinned and swung around, using his crutch as a pivot.

"And, Trace?" Hailey called after him.

"Yeah?"

"Tell Marten I'm glad he's alive."

When he hobbled out of the house, Hailey brushed her bangs back from her face. "I am glad he's alive, but I can't believe he staged that whole ferry accident. He knew what I'd think."

"Maybe that was his way of protecting you. If he were dead, then there's no way he could've told you what he knew about the setup of Denver." Joe stroked his chin. "What do you think he has planned?"

"I don't know, but he'd better speak up soon or this danger will continue to hang over us both."

Hailey packed a bag, including her toiletries and her evening gown for the fund-raiser.

When Joe saw the long dress draped over her bag, he swore. "In all the excitement, I forgot to pick up my tux."

"All taken care of. I called Tony when you were at your hotel, and he's having it delivered to the Pacific Rim. If you need him for a fitting, he'll be happy to come over to the hotel."

"The fit of my tux is the last thing on my mind." He pounded a fist against his chest. "As long as there's room for my shoulder holster."

"That request must've driven Tony nuts. It will definitely ruin the drape of the suit."

"Do you want your bodyguard to keep you safe or look good in his tux?"

She ran her hands across his chest. "Lucky me, I don't have to make that choice."

They loaded their bags in the trunk of the Jag and drove to the hotel.

As soon as Hailey checked in, her assistant, Gretchen Reynolds, appeared at her side. "I can't believe you're going through with this after what happened at the Pacific Heights house."

"Great to see you, too, Gretchen. This is Joe McVie. Joe, my assistant, Gretchen."

As they shook hands, Gretchen gave Joe the once-over. "He'd better be here to protect you."

"I am." Joe leaned close to Gretchen. "And I'm not the only one here in that capacity."

Gretchen's eyes bugged out. "Is the SFPD ramping up security because of what happened at the house?"

"Yes." Hailey patted Gretchen's hand. "Don't worry. Everything is under control, and you did a beautiful job. We're going to raise lots of money."

When they got up to the suite, Hailey slid open the closet door. "Tux is here. Do you want to try it on?"

"I'm sure it's fine, Hailey." Joe collapsed on the bed.

"You wanna give me the lowdown on the festivities tonight?"

"I'll take you to the ballroom where it's being held so you can look around." She hung up her dress in the closet. "At seven o'clock cocktails and hors d'oeuvres. A few speeches—none by Nurse Ayala Khan—buffet dinner, and then dancing and more cocktails."

"That's all *you* have planned, anyway, but what's planned for you?"

"Whatever it is, I'm sure you and the SFPD and maybe even Agent Porter will take care of it. Ayala has been outed."

"She's just the face we know. What about all the other faces we don't know? I'm sure there are others like her—outwardly dedicated to one cause and secretly supporting another."

"Whatever's gonna happen is gonna happen."

"Those forces of evil?"

She shrugged. A sense of calm had descended on her after she'd left the hospital. Maybe it was knowing Joe McVie was on her side. "I forwarded the guest list to the FBI."

"Recently?"

"Today."

"Hate to break it to you, but they don't work that fast. Don't tell Agent Porter I said that."

"My lips are sealed." She drew a finger over the seam of her lips. "Do you want me to give you a tour of the ballroom now?"

"Dinner at eight?" Joe rubbed his stomach. "I'm starving. Let's eat first and then I'll check it out."

"There are a couple of great restaurants in this hotel." Hailey reached for her purse.

"Room service." Joe bounded up from the bed and slid the embossed leather folder on the desk toward him. "We're eating in. The less exposure you have, the better. The danger is not over, Hailey, just because Ayala's on the run."

"I know that. It's coming. I feel it coming—but now I'm ready."

THE REST OF the afternoon passed with both of them working on their laptops. As day shifted into night, Joe stretched and rubbed his eyes.

Hailey looked up from her screen. "Are you in trouble?"

"What?" Folding his hands behind his head, Joe kicked his feet onto the desk next to his laptop.

"You've been awfully busy over there, typing away. Are you writing out your defense?" Hailey stretched out her legs on the bed and wiggled her bare toes.

"Answering some emails and, yeah, explaining myself."

"I repeat. Are you in trouble?"

"No." He spun his cell phone around to face him. "But we will be if we don't start getting ready for this damn gala."

"We have over an hour. I don't know about you, pretty boy, but I don't need that long to get ready."

Joe swung his legs off the desk and stalked toward the bed. "I do, when I plan to shower with my protectee and ravish her in the process."

Hailey shoved her computer off her lap. "Then what are we waiting for?"

Just about an hour later, completely sated and clean in the bargain, Joe faced the mirror in his monkey suit.

Hailey came up behind him, her shimmery silver dress floating around her legs. She reached around him and straightened his bow tie. "You look very handsome."

"You look—" he flicked the skirt of her dress "—stunning."

She kissed the side of his neck and then twirled away to snag his jacket from the back of a chair. "I'll help you into your jacket."

"First things first." He slid open the closet door and retrieved his shoulder holster. "You can help me into this before the jacket."

She sighed. "Poor Tony."

"It'll be fine."

After he strapped on his holster and secured his weapon, Hailey held out his jacket for him. He slipped into the jacket, and Hailey patted his chest.

"More than fine, Red. You're going to have to stick by me when we walk in, because I don't have a ticket for you. Gretchen sent one over and I thought I printed it out at the house, but with the sniper fire and bomb blast, who knows what happened to it?"

"I plan to stick very close to you."

As soon as they left the safety of the room, all of Joe's senses went on high alert. If someone wanted to take out Hailey or make some kind of statement about the war, this gala provided the perfect venue.

Damn that de Becker. What was he waiting for? The longer he kept quiet, the longer Hailey faced danger.

The guards at the door of the ballroom patted him down after Hailey told them he was with her and was providing personal security, so they skimmed over his weapon.

Joe blinked at the dazzling decor of the ballroom. This place couldn't be farther from that Syrian refugee camp. Maybe after the keynote address, all the wealth and comfort were supposed to make the guests feel guilty.

Hailey understood that.

Joe declined the champagne floating around on waiters' trays, but Hailey grabbed a glass of the bubbly and downed half of it before coming up for air.

"Is that a good idea?" Joe raised one eyebrow.

"You're the only one who has to stay sober, Red."

The guests began to filter in through the doors after being checked out by security, and the level of noise in the ballroom increased minute by minute.

Joe nodded toward Agent Porter, his football-player frame dressed to the nines. He was here as a guest, too, but he had his eyes wide-open.

Putting him firmly in the guest column, Hailey introduced Joe to her foundation's board members and acquaintances as a…friend. If the *friend* designation allowed him to continue doing all those things to her body that he'd just done in the hotel suite, he'd take it.

The dais at one end of the room sported a podium, long tables on either side and a screen behind it. Would images of the devastation in Syria be projected on that screen, or would that be going too far for this crowd?

A small commotion stirred around the side door to the right of the dais as two security guards ushered in a tall, lean man and two women.

Hailey followed his gaze and said, "That's Dr. Nabil Karam-Thomas and Dr. Lynne Roberson. The other woman is Dr. Roberson's date, I believe."

"Dr. Karam-Thomas, the keynote speaker."

"That's right. He's done a lot to recruit volunteers in the medical field."

"Thomas?"

"English father, Syrian mother, I believe." Hailey deposited her champagne flute on a passing tray. "They're coming this way."

As the small group approached, Hailey sailed forward, extending her hands. "I'm so happy you could make it tonight, and everyone is looking forward to your speech, Dr. Karam-Thomas."

"So good to see you again, Hailey, and please, call me Nabil."

"Dr. Roberson, welcome." Hailey took the woman's hand. "This is Joe McVie. Joe, Dr. Roberson and…"

Dr. Roberson gave Joe's hand a firm shake. "This is Valerie Guida."

After shaking hands with both of the women, Joe made a half turn toward Dr. Karam-Thomas.

"Nice to meet you, Valerie." Hailey turned toward Dr. Karam-Thomas. "Dr.—Nabil, this is Joe McVie. Joe, Dr. Nabil Karam-Thomas."

As Joe shook hands with the doctor, Karam-Thomas tightened his grip, his ring squeezing against Joe's knuckle. When they released, Joe glanced at the large gold band on the doctor's right hand. It looked like a wedding band that belonged on his left hand.

Joe glanced at Karam-Thomas's left hand and cocked his head. The ring on the doctor's third finger boasted a red stone, unusual for its dark color. Where had he seen a stone like that recently?

He slid a gaze at Hailey's hands, expressively gesturing as she spoke to the doctors, her long fingers adorned with three diamond rings. The lady obviously preferred diamonds to rubies, or whatever that stone was.

Joe tuned back into the conversation just in time to hear Dr. Roberson ask about Ayala Khan.

"I've heard great things about the work Ayala does at the refugee center near the Turkish border. Will she be here tonight, Hailey?"

Hailey pinched the sleeve of Joe's jacket. "Sh-she wasn't able to make it."

Not done singing Ayala's praises, Dr. Roberson turned to Dr. Karam-Thomas. "Have you met Ayala Khan, Nabil? She's Syrian, too."

Karam-Thomas flashed his easy smile and held

up his hands. "I can claim only half Syrian ancestry. I have not met Ms. Khan, but I've heard wonderful things about her. Maybe next time our paths will cross."

"Hailey——" Joe held up a finger "—I thought you said Dr. Karam-Thomas had visited the refugee center when you were working there. Wouldn't he have met Ayala then?"

Hailey's body stiffened next to his.

She obviously didn't want to put a damper on the evening by announcing that one of the Syrian Florence Nightingales was fomenting terror and destruction, and he had no intention of outing her now. He just thought it strange that Karam-Thomas wouldn't have remembered meeting Ayala. The guy was probably too much the superstar to remember all the underlings.

"That's right." The doctor snapped the fingers of his left hand, and the red stone caught the light and glinted. "I *did* meet Ms. Khan on that visit—amazing nurse. Now, if you ladies and gentleman will excuse me, I'm going to press some flesh."

"That would be advisable." Hailey swept her hand to the side as if to make a path for him.

Joe watched Karam-Thomas's ramrod-straight back as he melted into the glittering crowd, glad-handing and probably flashing that smile. "That's weird."

"What?"

"That he didn't remember meeting Ayala."

"Why?" Hailey smiled and wiggled her fingers at

Dr. Roberson and her companion as they moved away to mingle. "Why are you even bringing her up?"

"I didn't. Dr. Roberson did."

"But why call out Dr. Karam-Thomas like that? I don't want her involvement in the bombing of the center to come out here, of all places."

"I'm sorry, Hailey. I just remembered that conversation we had with Ayala when you mentioned he was going to be the keynote speaker and thought it was odd he didn't remember her."

"Not really." She tipped her head toward the doctor, who was in the center of a group of adoring fans. "He's a very popular and busy guy. Speaking of which, I need to make some opening remarks before the food and Nabil's address."

Hailey's speech seemed to go smoothly. Joe didn't comprehend one word of it as he watched the crowd, his senses alert to every cough and scrape of a chair leg.

The audience met Dr. Karam-Thomas's speech with resounding applause, and Joe's muscles relaxed—just a tad. The evening seemed to be progressing without a hitch…and without any attempts on Hailey's life.

The knots in Joe's gut prevented him from enjoying or even eating much dinner. Hailey had wanted him up on that dais with her and the doctors and several Syrian dignitaries, but Joe felt more comfortable roaming the crowd.

As dinner began to wind down and the coffee was served, a ruckus erupted at the entrance to the ballroom. Joe went on high alert, pushed off the wall where he'd been leaning and strode toward the noise.

Two security guards held a struggling man between them—a man wearing a black porkpie hat with a checkered band.

"Let me in. Tell Hailey Duvall who I am. She'll know."

Agent Porter sidled up next to Joe. "I'll be damned. It's Marten de Becker."

Joe whistled. "And this is the venue he's chosen for his reveal—public and safe."

Porter made a move. He badged the security guards. "Let him through. Ms. Duvall is going to want to see him, and even more, she's going to want to hear what he has to say. We all do."

Security released de Becker, and he brushed off his clothes and tipped his hat at Joe when he sauntered by under Porter's protective watch.

Joe followed them up to the dais.

When Hailey saw de Becker, she jumped up from her chair and lifted the skirt of her dress to jog down the steps to the ballroom floor. She threw her arms around him and whispered something in his ear.

Joe clenched his jaw. She'd better be telling him to get up there and spill his guts once and for all.

While the other notables on the dais continued eating their desserts and drinking their coffee, Dr. Karam-Thomas had eased out of his chair and headed toward the opposite side of the dais from where Hailey was still talking to de Becker…even though the doctor's seat was steps away from them on the same side.

Joe watched his descent from the stage through narrowed eyes. Karam-Thomas seemed to be in a hurry without trying to appear he was in a hurry—and that megawatt smile had disappeared.

The doctor slipped one hand in his pocket—the right hand—and once again, Joe caught a glimpse of that unusual ring. The same ring Ayala wore on her left hand.

Adrenaline surged through Joe's body, and he lurched forward to follow Karam-Thomas as he wove his way through the tables, barely acknowledging his admirers as they reached out to him.

Why did he have his hand bunched in his pocket? That small space couldn't accommodate a gun—even a small one.

Joe slipped his hand beneath his jacket to grip the handle of his own weapon as he continued to follow the doctor, who was completely unaware he had a tail.

Joe planned to keep it that way. He circled around to the right, keeping Karam-Thomas in his sights.

When Hailey's voice boomed over the speaker system, the doctor tripped to a stop and cranked his head over his shoulder.

"We have a surprise guest tonight, someone who worked in Syria with me, and he'd like to say a few words."

Karam-Thomas's feet seemed rooted to the floor, his face a white oval as he listened to Hailey's introduction of Marten de Becker. Then he lurched forward, not even trying to mask his hurried pace.

Joe continued circling to the doctor's right.

Karam-Thomas pulled his hand from his pocket, and Joe focused on the way the doctor's fingers curled around the device in his hand, his thumb positioned on the top of the item.

Joe drew closer, and his heart slammed against his rib cage as he recognized a remote clutched in the doctor's hand, his thumb pressing against the release.

Joe knew those triggers. Once the doctor released his thumb, it would set off an explosive device. But where was the device? Was this a suicide mission for the doc? Did he have something strapped to his body?

Hailey's voice carried across the ballroom. "So, I'd like to turn over the microphone to my fellow aid worker in Syria, Marten de Becker."

Applause rippled through the ballroom as de Becker approached the podium.

Licking his lips, Dr. Karam-Thomas glanced over his right shoulder. As Marten began his speech, the doctor lurched toward the exit, his hand wrapped around the remote.

A deadly calm descended on Joe as he made his decision. In four long steps he reached the doctor's side before he got to the exit door.

With his left hand, Joe grabbed the doctor's hand clutching the device and covered his thumb with his own, pressing down on the release with all his strength.

Karam-Thomas bucked under the assault. He dipped

his left hand in his pocket, and a knife flashed before a searing pain ran up Joe's thigh.

Gritting his teeth, Joe squeezed the doctor's hand in a death grip, raised the gun to his temple and growled, "You're not ruining this party."

Then he pulled the trigger.

Chapter Fifteen

The gunfire echoed in the ballroom…and in Joe's ears. People screamed and ducked.

De Becker shouted into the mic, "Get down, get down."

Karam-Thomas jerked once and then his body slumped, heavy against Joe's, his head falling to the side, blood running down his face and soaking Joe's jacket. The doctor's hand holding the remote began to slip from his, and Joe crushed the dead man's fingers, repositioning his thumb over Karam-Thomas's.

As a security guard rushed him, Joe dropped his gun and wrapped his arm around the doctor's chest. He could either prop him up in a macabre dance or hit the ground with him. Then he had no choice. As Karam-Thomas slipped to the floor, Joe had to go with him, every ounce of his energy focused on covering the doctor's thumb with his own.

He fell on top of the body. A gun clicked in his ear, and a boot kicked him in the back. "Get off him. Roll over."

"Can't do that." A bead of sweat rolled down Joe's

face and hung off his chin. He raised his arm, his hand still engulfing Karam-Thomas's and the remote, his thumb going numb with the pressure. "Once this trigger is released, something's gonna blow—I don't know where it is or what it is, but this death switch is the key. Get everyone out of here. Find FBI agent Porter and evacuate. Now."

Another security agent joined the first one. "I know who Agent Porter is. I'll get him, but keep your weapon trained on him. We don't know what's going on."

People began streaming past Joe and the dead man beneath him, giving them a wide berth. Blood covered the front of his shirt, and the leg of his trouser sported a rip from the knife Karam-Thomas had swung at him. Tony would never forgive him.

He shouted to the security guard, "Direct these people to the other exits, for God's sake. They don't need to see this."

Seconds later, Hailey crouched beside him, the hem of her sparkly dress brushing the pool of blood on the floor. "Oh my God, Joe. What happened? You're not telling me Nabil planted a bomb in the ballroom. How did you know what he was planning?"

"His ring. Look at his ring, Hailey. It's the same one Ayala had. They're a couple. He probably recruited her. Hell, they might even be married, for all we know."

Hailey choked and then scrambled to her feet. Was she overwhelmed by guilt and remorse for trusting those two? For inviting Dr. Karam-Thomas into this world? She had to stop doing that to herself. People took advantage of her because she had a kind and giving heart—he hoped she'd never change.

Less than a minute later, Hailey returned with several white napkins from the tables. She pressed them against the wound on his thigh. "Your leg is bleeding. How long are you going to have to hold down that button?"

"As long as it takes." Porter loomed above them. "Good work, McVie. How long *can* you hold on? The bomb squad is on its way."

"Like you said, Porter. As long as it takes."

De Becker joined the crowd encircling Joe and Karam-Thomas's inert form. "Damn, I didn't even get to talk."

Joe growled low in his throat. "This is your fault, de Becker. Why did you lie about Major Denver in the first place?"

"Money and intrigue." De Becker straightened his hat. "Money first, I'll admit, but I was able to draw out the terrorist group behind the bombing and behind the setup of Denver. Isn't that worth something to you?"

"Not as much as Hailey's life."

She leaned forward and kissed him—dead guy and all.

Ten minutes later the ballroom had been cleared and the bomb squad arrived with explosive-sniffing dogs.

A member of the team leaned over Joe and slid a device between the doctor's thumb and the remote to keep the trigger in place. "You can release now, buddy. Amazing job."

Joe rolled onto his back, shook out his hand and flexed his fingers. "Why didn't I have one of those?"

Hailey crouched beside him and waved her arm in the air. "Hey, did someone bother to call an ambulance? Joe's been stabbed in the leg."

"It's nothing. He barely got me."

Porter said, "Police and EMTs are out front. A few people got hurt in the scramble to get out of here, and they're being treated at a triage center away from the hotel. The entire hotel is being evacuated."

One of the German shepherds started barking furiously at the front of the ballroom.

"We got a hit. Let's move these people out of here."

Agent Porter and Hailey helped Joe to his feet, and he limped out of the ballroom between them. They moved toward the curved staircase that led from the lobby to the ballroom.

When Joe spotted de Becker on the top step, his blood boiled all over again. He had put everyone's life in danger playing his stupid spy games.

A woman stepped up beside de Becker, and Joe stumbled to a halt as Hailey gasped.

"Ayala!"

"What have you done? What have you done with Nabil?" The gun she held to Marten's head trembled in her hand.

"It's over, Ayala." Joe struggled forward as both Hailey and Porter held him back. "Nabil's dead. The bomb squad has located the explosive device. Your plan failed."

Her dark eyes flashed. "It's not over. We have more people than you can even dream of for our cause. People you trust."

"But not Major Denver. You lied about him. You lied about his presence at the kidnapping. Why? Why him?"

Ayala laughed. "You're wrong. We do have Major Denver."

De Becker took a step away from Ayala. "That's not true. I was paid to lie about hearing Denver there and then threatened when I decided to tell the truth."

"You don't know anything, Marten."

Ayala's weapon had slipped an inch or two, and Joe nudged Porter.

"Our cause will continue with the help of people like Denver…and others."

"What is your cause, Ayala?" Hailey reached out a hand. "I thought we shared the same cause—to help innocents affected by war."

"Short-term casualties for a long-term goal, Hailey. You will never understand our goal."

"Try me." Hailey edged away from Joe toward Ayala as he made a grab for her hand.

Now was not the time for philanthropy.

"And you will never understand our commitment to it." She cried out, "Nabil!"

Then she turned the gun on herself.

Epilogue

Hailey joined Joe at the window, curled her arms around his waist and drank in the view of the San Francisco Bay. "It's a beautiful day for January."

"It might be sunny, but it's still cold." He twisted his head over his shoulder and kissed her mouth. "Let's go back to bed."

"Oh, no, you don't, Red. We've been in bed for the past two days while it's been cloudy and raining." She patted his bandaged thigh. "Time to stretch out that leg."

"You're a stern taskmaster. I just took down a terrorist, shooting him in the head and hanging on to that detonator for dear life as he fell to the floor." He wove his fingers through hers. "Don't I deserve a break?"

"You're lucky that was a detonator in Nabil's hand and not a remote control for the projector."

"I had it and him all figured out by the time I took him down. When I recognized that ring, I knew he was the one who recruited Ayala at that symposium in Florida. They were lovers, shared the same ring, shared the same passion—a passion for destruction."

"Agent Porter showed me video footage from the hotel of a woman, who I ID'd for him as Ayala, using a ticket to the gala to get into the ballroom. That's when she set up the explosives beneath the dais, but did she and the doctor know Marten was going to show up?"

"I think that was just icing on the cake for them. They planned to disrupt that fund-raiser one way or another, with or without de Becker there. Maybe Karam-Thomas's hand was forced when de Becker showed up, and he sped up the timeline."

"I'm just glad you were suspicious of the doctor and kept an eye on him. I never would've guessed he'd be involved in trying to block a peace process in Syria."

"Why would you? The guy was smooth."

"And Marten got to make his announcement in public, just like he wanted."

"Clearing Major Denver of any involvement in that bombing, despite what Ayala claimed."

Hailey smoothed a thumb over the crease between his eyebrows. "Doesn't that make you happy?"

"It does, but Denver's still out there. He has no way of knowing we've been slowly chipping away at the evidence against him. I just wish there were some way we could reach him. If he came in now, he might have a chance of completely clearing his name."

"The CIA and the army still believe he's in league with a terrorist group, and Ayala's statements before her death didn't help matters."

"They do believe that, but now we'll have a better idea of which group it is as the CIA and the FBI start to sort through Nabil's connections. I did believe one part of Ayala's admission before she ended her life."

"That we'd never understand their cause?"

"No. That they have people in high places on their side."

"Those people will be exposed eventually." Hailey slipped between Joe and the window and rested her hands on his broad shoulders. "Now it's back to work for you, isn't it?"

"Once my leg heals." He cupped her face with his hands. "Are you going to wait for me? Because I'm telling you right now, Hailey Duvall, I can't live without you."

"Of course I'll wait. I love you." Turning her head to the side, she kissed his palm. "But if you think I'm going to be cooling my heels on a tennis court or sipping mimosas at brunch during your next deployment, you've got the wrong socialite, Red."

He rolled his eyes. "Where this time?"

"I thought I'd play it safe and volunteer to build some homes in Guatemala."

"Just as long as there are no bombs involved."

"I would hope not." She broke away from his embrace. "Right now, though, I'm not averse to sipping a couple of mimosas."

"In bed?"

His hopeful tone brought a smile to her lips.

"One-track mind." She tapped her temple. "I was thinking of this little place in Big Sur, but I need a driver."

"I'm your man." He saluted.

"Good, because there's a '66 T-Bird in the garage, and it's been cooped up a little too long—just like a redheaded D-Boy I know."

Joe's eyes, as blue as the bay behind him, lit up. "That offer just might be better than sex."

"Watch yourself." She shook her finger at him. "Of course, if we see any needy people on our way out of the city, we might have to stop and help them or maybe even take them along with us. Would that be a problem?"

He reached out and pulled her into his arms again. As he nuzzled her neck, he murmured, "Do-gooder."

* * * * *

*Look for more books in Carol Ericson's
Red, White and Built: Pumped Up
miniseries, later in 2019.*

*And don't miss the previous titles in the
Red, White and Built: Pumped Up series:*

Delta Force Defender
Delta Force Daddy

Available now from Harlequin Intrigue!

Get 4 FREE REWARDS!

We'll send you 2 FREE Books plus 2 FREE Mystery Gifts.

Harlequin Intrigue® books feature heroes and heroines that confront and survive danger while finding themselves irresistibly drawn to one another.

FREE
Value Over
$20

YES! Please send me 2 FREE Harlequin Intrigue® novels and my 2 FREE gifts (gifts are worth about $10 retail). After receiving them, if I don't wish to receive any more books, I can return the shipping statement marked "cancel." If I don't cancel, I will receive 6 brand-new novels every month and be billed just $4.99 each for the regular-print edition or $5.74 each for the larger-print edition in the U.S., or $5.74 each for the regular-print edition or $6.49 each for the larger-print edition in Canada. That's a savings of at least 12% off the cover price! It's quite a bargain! Shipping and handling is just 50¢ per book in the U.S. and 75¢ per book in Canada.* I understand that accepting the 2 free books and gifts places me under no obligation to buy anything. I can always return a shipment and cancel at any time. The free books and gifts are mine to keep no matter what I decide.

Choose one: ☐ **Harlequin Intrigue®**
                Regular-Print
                (182/382 HDN GMYW)

☐ **Harlequin Intrigue®**
   Larger-Print
   (199/399 HDN GMYW)

Name (please print)

Address   Apt. #

City   State/Province   Zip/Postal Code

Mail to the **Reader Service:**
IN U.S.A.: P.O. Box 1341, Buffalo, NY 14240-8531
IN CANADA: P.O. Box 603, Fort Erie, Ontario L2A 5X3

Want to try 2 free books from another series! Call 1-800-873-8635 or visit www.ReaderService.com.

---

*Terms and prices subject to change without notice. Prices do not include sales taxes, which will be charged (if applicable) based on your state or country of residence. Canadian residents will be charged applicable taxes. Offer not valid in Quebec. This offer is limited to one order per household. Books received may not be as shown. Not valid for current subscribers to Harlequin Intrigue books. All orders subject to approval. Credit or debit balances in a customer's account(s) may be offset by any other outstanding balance owed by or to the customer. Please allow 4 to 6 weeks for delivery. Offer available while quantities last.

Your Privacy—The Reader Service is committed to protecting your privacy. Our Privacy Policy is available online at www.ReaderService.com or upon request from the Reader Service. We make a portion of our mailing list available to reputable third parties that offer products we believe may interest you. If you prefer that we not exchange your name with third parties, or if you wish to clarify or modify your communication preferences, please visit us at www.ReaderService.com/consumerschoice or write to us at Reader Service Preference Service, P.O. Box 9062, Buffalo, NY 14240-9062. Include your complete name and address.

HI19R

I N T R I G U E

*Audrey Anderson will do whatever it takes to keep her
family's newspaper running. Following a murder in
town, Audrey must break the story, despite the fact that
doing so will put her at risk. Can Sheriff Colt Tanner
keep her out of trouble—or will their reignited love
cause them to face even more danger?*

Read on for a sneak preview of In Self Defense,
*a thrilling new romantic suspense novel from
USA TODAY bestselling author Debra Webb.*

Franklin County, Tennessee
Monday, February 25, 9:10 p.m.

The red-and-blue lights flashed in the night.

Audrey Anderson opened her car door and stepped out
onto the gravel road. She grimaced and wished she'd taken
time to change her shoes, but time was not an available luxury
when the police scanner spit out the code for a shooting that
ended in a call to the coroner. Good thing her dedicated editor,
Brian Peterson, had his ear to the police radio pretty much
24/7 and immediately texted her.

The sheriff's truck was already on-site, along with two
county cruisers and the coroner's van. So far no news vans
and no cars that she noticed belonging to other reporters
from the tri-county area. Strange, that cocky reporter from
the *Tullahoma Telegraph* almost always arrived on the scene
before Audrey. Maybe she had a friend in the department.

Then again, Audrey had her own sources, too. She reached
back into the car for her bag. So far the closest private source
she had was the sheriff himself—which was only because he
still felt guilty for cheating on her back in high school.

Audrey was not above using that guilt whenever the need
arose.

Tonight seemed like the perfect time to remind the man she'd once thought she would marry that he owed her one or two or a hundred.

She shuddered as the cold night air sent a shiver through her. Late February was marked by all sorts of lovely blooms and promises of spring, but it was all just an illusion. It was still winter and Mother Nature loved letting folks know who was boss. Like tonight—the gorgeous sixty-two-degree sunny day had turned into a bone-chilling evening. Audrey shivered, wishing she'd worn a coat to dinner.

Buncombe Road snaked through a farming community situated about halfway between Huntland and Winchester— every agricultural mile fell under the Franklin County sheriff's jurisdiction. The houses, mostly farmhouses sitting amid dozens if not hundreds of acres of pastures and fields, were scattered few and far between. But that wasn't the surprising part of the location. This particular house and farm belonged to a Mennonite family. Rarely did violence or any other sort of trouble within this quiet, closed community ripple beyond its boundaries. Most issues were handled privately and silently. The Mennonites kept to themselves for the most part and never bothered anyone. A few operated public businesses within the local community, and most interactions were kept strictly within the business domain. There was no real intermingling or socializing within the larger community— not even Winchester, which was the county seat and buzzed with activity.

Whatever happened inside this turn-of-the-nineteenth-century farmhouse tonight was beyond the closed community's ability to settle amid their own ranks.

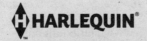